STINETINGLERS 2

10 MORE New Stories
by the
Master of Scary Tales

R.L. STINE

FEIWEL AND FRIENDS
NEW YORK

To Jean Feiwel,

who made me SCARY!

A Feiwel and Friends Book

An imprint of Macmillan Publishing Group, LLC

120 Broadway, New York, NY 10271 • mackids.com

Our books may be purchased in bulk for promotional, educational, or business use. Please contact your local bookseller or the Macmillan Corporate and Premium Sales Department at (800) 221-7945 ext. 5442 or by email at MacmillanSpecialMarkets@macmillan.com.

Library of Congress Cataloging-in-Publication Data is available.

First edition, 2023

Book design by Trisha Previte and L. Whitt

Feiwel and Friends logo designed by Filomena Tuosto

Printed in the United States of America by Lakeside Book Company

ISBN 978-1-250-83631-1 (hardcover)

10 9 8 7 6 5 4 3 2 1

ISBN 978-1-250-32156-5 (special edition)

10 9 8 7 6 5 4 3 2 1

CONTENTS

INTRODUCTION

You're afraid of spiders, and suddenly, you start seeing them everywhere—even in your salad.

Those noises you keep hearing? You begin to suspect someone is living inside your wall.

Your good-luck charm seems to be bringing you bad luck. Are you really being chased by a herd of elephants?

You love your new stopwatch—until it stops time. Now you are trapped in time—and no one can hear you or come to help.

Those are some of the stories in this book. None of them could happen to you—could they?

I wrote these ten new stories to give you a chill.

You know. That tingle you get all over your body when you start to feel afraid.

I hope my new stories take you to a Stinetingling world of fantasy and fear, shadows and fright.

Reader, beware. That cold tingle may become a SCREAM!

LUCKY ME

When I was a kid, a lot of people carried around a rabbit's foot on a little chain for good luck. I don't know how a rabbit's foot could bring good luck. It certainly wasn't lucky for the rabbit!

My brother Bill had a rabbit's foot that he carried in his pocket at all times. He really believed it was a good-luck charm.

One day I decided to play a mean trick on Bill. I took his rabbit's foot and I hid it under a pile of clothes in the bottom dresser drawer. The next morning, he looked everywhere for it. He was very upset that he had to go to school without the rabbit's foot.

That afternoon, he fell in a hole on the playground and broke his wrist.

I felt terrible. I knew it was all my fault. I stuffed the rabbit's foot back in his jeans when he wasn't looking. But, of course, it was too late.

I never forgot that unlucky trick I played on Bill. And I thought of it when I wrote this story.

I DIDN'T FALL INTO THE ELEPHANT HABITAT. I JUMPED.

I was walking with Mom and Dad along Elephant Row. We were following the arrows to the penguin house when a burst of wind blew the cap off my head.

I made a grab for it, but it sailed high and then swooped over the wall into the elephant preserve. My favorite baseball cap! I couldn't afford to lose it.

Dad grabbed my arm and tried to hold me back. He knew what I was about to do.

"Let go!" I screamed and broke free. And I leaped onto the high fence. I'm not a great athlete. But I timed it right and got lucky.

I caught the top of the fence with both hands and hoisted myself over the side.

I could hear Mom and Dad shouting on the other side of the fence. And then, other zoo visitors were shouting, too. But *no way* could I lose my best baseball cap. I wore it all the time, sometimes even in bed.

The afternoon sun flashed in my eyes. I blinked and gazed around, struggling to find the cap. It didn't take long to spot it. It had come to rest at the bottom of a low clump of weeds.

"I see it!" I shouted as loud as I could. I thought maybe that would calm down my screaming parents on the other side of the fence. But they kept crying out and calling to me.

"Get out of there!"

"Chuck—get out of there! Now!"

I cupped my hands around my mouth and yelled, "I'll be right out!"

Blinking, I shielded my eyes with one elbow and darted toward the cap. I couldn't get the sun out of my eyes.

I saw the blue cap clearly, resting against the brown weeds. But I didn't see the elephant charging over the grass.

My legs were kind of shaky and I could feel my heart ticking in my chest. I knew I didn't have time to think about how scary this was. I had to grab the cap, spin around, and make the leap back to safety.

I didn't see the elephant until it was too late.

I mean, I heard a shrill roar as I bent down for the baseball cap. The cap dropped from my hand, and I gazed up in time to see the elephant thundering toward me.

Did he plan to knock me over and then crush me into the ground?

I didn't really have time to think about what the huge animal was planning. And I knew I couldn't explain to him that I didn't mean to invade his territory. I just needed my cap back.

So I swiped the cap and rolled. The old tuck-and-roll. I'm not sure where I learned it.

The big elephant roared past me and crashed headfirst into the fence.

Was he going to turn and charge again?

I don't know. I was already at the top of the fence, scrambling to safety on the other side.

Dad was angry. Mom was crying. She hugged me and wouldn't let go.

I jammed the cap tightly over my head and squirmed away from her.

"You were lucky," Dad muttered.

"We're always lucky," I said.

Frowning, Dad pulled the lucky charm from under his shirt. He wears it inside a small black velvet bag around his neck. He never takes it off.

He tugged the charm from the bag and held it out to me. I kissed it, and he slid it back into the bag. Then he tucked it under his shirt.

I got the lucky charm for my parents two weeks ago. I

know we'll be lucky from now on. Even when I'm attacked by an elephant in the zoo, I will be okay.

I should explain some things. To start, I have to tell you that our last name is Lucky.

Actually, Dad's last name was Luchow. Lewis Luchow. But when he married Mom, he said he was the luckiest man on earth. He went to a lawyer, and he had their last name changed to Lucky.

Mom is Hannah Lucky. My little sister is Emma Lucky. And I am Charles Lucky. Unfortunately, everyone has always called me Chuck. You've got it. Chuck Lucky.

I hate the name. I take a lot of teasing from everyone. Some kids at school started calling me Chuckles. Luckily, that didn't last long.

Emma called me Chuckles for a long time, just to be annoying. So you know what I did? I went into her room and turned the heads backward on all her panda bears.

She hasn't called me Chuckles ever since.

Anyway, luck has always played a very big part in our family. Dad always says, "The Luckys are the luckiest people we know."

I never like to brag. But I am the main reason we are so lucky. That's because I'm the one who brought home the lucky charm.

I had been saving up my allowance because I wanted to buy Mom and Dad a present for their birthday.

They were both born on May first. They have the same birthday. How lucky is that?

I had saved almost thirty dollars. But I didn't know what to buy them. They collect old jewelry, and they're always spending time in antique stores. I knew I couldn't afford to buy anything there.

Then one afternoon, Dad was late picking me up after my tennis lesson at the Sports Center downtown. I spotted a tiny store across the street and walked over to it.

The front window was filled with all kinds of strange objects. Carved heads, and beads carved out of bone, and shiny, old-looking rings and earrings, and animal pins, tiny skulls, rubber snakes, and two small rabbits. I couldn't tell if they were real or stuffed.

I raised my eyes to the sign above the glass door. ODD THINGS. That's what the store was called. And then something shiny in the corner of the window caught my eyes. And I thought maybe I'd found a good gift for Mom and Dad.

A bell rang as I pulled open the door and stepped inside. There was bright sunshine outside, but the store was nearly dark as night. I squinted into the gray light and shadows, waiting for my eyes to adjust.

I realized I was shivering. It was a warm spring day. But the store was cold as a refrigerator. The air felt heavy and damp.

I heard a cough. The sound startled me, and I dropped my tennis racket. It clattered at my feet. I bent to pick it up, and a soft, croaky voice said, "I am Mr. Fogg. Can I help you, young man?"

I stood up and saw the man leaning on the glass counter in front of me. He appeared old, with scraggly white hair that fell over his forehead, a wrinkled, pruney face, gray stubbly whiskers on his cheeks.

His eyes made me freeze. They were bright blue. Blue as the sky, and they glowed in the darkness of the store.

"I—I saw something in the window," I stammered.

Mr. Fogg moved out from behind the counter. He held a cane that he tapped in front of him as he made his way slowly to the window. I followed him and pointed to the shiny object I had seen.

"The good-luck charm," he said. His voice was a rough whisper. He plucked it from the window and carried it to the counter, tapping his cane as he walked.

I stared down at it. It was shiny metal, about the size of a baseball card. "Good-luck charm?" I said. "For real?"

He nodded. "Everything in my store is real," he said. He spun the charm between his fingers. "Do you recognize the shape, son?"

I shook my head. "Some kind of leaf?"

"It's a shamrock," he said. "Shamrocks are the only real

7

good-luck charms." Mr. Fogg turned it over so I could see the back. The words *Lucky Charm* appeared to be stenciled in black there.

I knew Mom and Dad would love this charm.

"How much does it cost?" I asked.

He closed his eyes. The glowing blue light appeared to go out. "I can't give it to just anyone," he said. "It's too real and too special."

"But it's a perfect gift for my parents," I said. "Our name is Lucky."

He opened his eyes and locked them on me. "Your name?"

"Yes," I said. "We're the Lucky family. I . . . I'm Charles Lucky."

The eyes burned into me. He was studying me, trying to see if I was telling the truth. "If your name is Lucky, you should have the charm. But I can't sell it to you, Charles," he said in his choked whisper.

"You can't?"

"I can only *give* it to you," he replied. "It's bad luck to sell it. And once you give it to your mom or dad as a present, they must wear it at all times for the charm to work."

My mind was spinning. *Is he really going to GIVE it to me? Can it be an actual good-luck charm? It really works?*

He gazed at me for a long time. His eyes glowed like headlights, so bright in the dark store. Finally, a long sigh escaped his lips. "Okay," he whispered. "I will give it to you."

"Oh, thank you!" I cried.

The shamrock gleamed in his hand. He opened a drawer behind the counter. His hand fumbled around inside it. He pulled out a small black velvet bag with a drawstring at the opening.

He slid the charm into the bag and pulled the string tight. Then he handed it to me over the counter.

"Mr. Fogg, is there any way I can pay you?" I asked.

He nodded. "Yes. You can pay me by having a lifetime of good luck."

I didn't know how to answer that. "I . . . I'll try," I blurted out.

I gripped the bag tightly in my hand. Then I turned and walked out of the store. The bell jangled behind me.

I stepped into the street and was hit by a car.

I sat up in bed, blinking at the bright lights. I gazed at the white walls all around me, trying to focus, to pull myself out of a haze.

Mom's smiling face floated over me. She had tears at the sides of her eyes. "You were lucky, Chuck," she said. Her voice trembled.

Dad appeared beside her. He had a wide smile on his face, too. "Only a few cuts and scrapes," he said.

I blinked some more. "Where am I?" I demanded. "In a hospital?"

They both nodded.

"A car hit you," Emma said.

I hadn't seen my sister. She sat in a chair against the wall.

"Why didn't you watch where you were going?" she asked.

Dad turned to her. "Don't give Chuck a hard time, Emma. He just had a close call."

"I can't believe how lucky you were," Mom repeated, letting the tears run down her cheeks.

That reminded me of the lucky charm. I sat up and gazed around the room. "Where is it?" I said. "Did you see a black bag?"

Dad pulled it from his pants pocket and held it in front of me. "You mean this? You were carrying it when you were hit by the car."

I felt so happy to see it. "It . . . it's a present," I said. "For you and Mom. For your birthday."

"A present?" Mom replied. "What is it?"

"It's the reason that car didn't hurt me," I explained. "Go ahead. Take it out of the bag."

Dad slid the shiny metal charm from the bag and held it up so Mom could see it.

"What is it? A bottle opener?" Emma chimed in. "That's a weird present."

"It's a shamrock," Dad said.

"Very pretty," Mom said.

"It's not an ordinary shamrock," I told them. "It's a good-luck charm. A real one. That car didn't hurt me because I was carrying it."

Dad turned it over and read the words on the back: *Lucky Charm*.

"Let me see it," Emma said. She jumped off the chair, darted to my bed, and grabbed it from Dad's hand.

"Oops." She dropped it and it clattered to the floor.

"Careful with it!" I cried. "It's not a toy! It's real—"

Dad gently pushed me back onto the pillow. "Don't get excited, Chuck. Emma won't hurt it."

She picked it up off the floor and handed it back to Dad. "Weird present," she repeated.

"It's a wonderful present," Mom said. "Thank you, Chuck."

"You have to wear it," I told Dad. "And never take it off."

"Huh? Okay. I'll do it." He slid the charm into the bag. Then he lowered the string around his neck and tucked the bag under his T-shirt. He laughed. "I'm feeling lucky already! Let's get the doctor to check you out, and we'll bring you home."

My neck ached a little, and I had a few cuts on my legs. But I didn't care. I knew the charm had worked its magic. I was okay. And I couldn't wait to get home.

"The Lucky family is going to be lucky from now on!" Mom declared.

Two weeks later, the charm protected me from the stampeding elephant at the zoo. As we drove home, I felt so proud that I had brought such good luck to my whole family.

But when we turned onto our block, a cloud of black smoke washed over the car. "What's burning?" Emma asked, sniffing the air. "I smell something burning."

Mom sniffed. "I smell it, too."

Another burst of black smoke covered our windshield. When it blew away, our house came into view.

"Ohhhh!" I cried out when I saw black smoke pouring from the roof, and red-orange flames darting from the front windows. "Our house is on fire!"

Dad slammed on the brakes. The car jerked to a stop at the curb.

He threw open the car door. "Rusty!" he cried. "Rusty is inside!"

I gasped again. A heavy feeling of dread washed over me.

Rusty. Our dog, trapped inside the burning house.

Dad was halfway up the front lawn, running hard. I heaved open my car door and chased after him. So frightened my legs weighed a hundred pounds each. I couldn't breathe.

"Rusty!" Dad shouted. "Rusty! We're coming!"

His voice was drowned out by the roar of the fire.

I jumped at a loud crash. Part of the roof fell in.

"Rusty! Rusty!"

I heard sirens in the distance. Someone must have called the fire department.

Dad reached the front door. Flames danced from the windows on both sides. He lowered his shoulder—and pushed the door in.

The door swung in, and Rusty came running out.

"Rusty—you're okay!" I cried. I reached out my arms to catch him in a hug.

But the little dog was in a panic. He ran right past me. "Rusty? Rusty?"

He ran to the street, nearly flying, and kept going. Rusty galloped full speed along the curb and disappeared into the woods at the end of the block.

I stood there screaming his name. I didn't stop till I felt Dad's hand on my shoulder. "We'll get him back, Chuck," he said. "At least we know he's okay."

Mom came up the lawn, shaking her head. "We were so lucky," she said. "We got back in time to save Rusty."

Dad pulled the shamrock from the bag. "Let's all kiss the lucky charm," he said. "It brought us enough luck to save Rusty's life."

We kissed the shamrock. Then Dad slid it back under his shirt.

Was it a real good-luck charm? I wanted to believe in it.

But as I watched the firefighters working to put out the flames, I began to have the tiniest doubt.

Mom and Dad found an apartment for us to live in while our house was being rebuilt.

"It's a little far from your school," Mom said. "But we were lucky to find it."

"It's too small," Emma said. "Why do Chuck and I have to share a room?"

"You have to count your luck where you get it," Dad said. "We're all safe and healthy." He pulled out the lucky shamrock and we all kissed it.

I decided to make a sign for my new room. I wanted to describe how I felt. I cut a square of wood with one of Dad's saws, and I painted the words LUCKY ME on the front in red paint.

I decided to nail it to the wall at the side of my bed. I started to pound in the first nail. "OWWWWWW!" I screamed as the hammer slipped and the nail went right through my palm.

Mom and Dad heard my howls of pain from the front room and came running. Dad grabbed my hand and held it. Mom's hand trembled, but she pulled the nail out quickly.

Wave after wave of throbbing pain shot down my arm.

Mom wrapped a bandage carefully around the hand.

"That's going to hurt for a while," Dad said. "But you were very lucky, Chuck."

"Huh? Lucky?" I cried.

He stared at the wound on the back of my hand. "Yes. Lucky," he said. "The nail didn't go through a vein. The bleeding is slowing down already."

He pulled the charm from under his shirt, and the three of us kissed it.

When they left the room, I slid the LUCKY ME sign under the bed. I didn't want to hang it up anymore.

Our neighbors found Rusty two days later. He was wandering in the woods. When they brought him to us, he was dirty and covered in leaves.

"That's so lucky you found him," Mom said.

Dad took out the good-luck charm and we all kissed it.

But Rusty wasn't really the same. He didn't wag his tail whenever he saw us. And when we threw a tennis ball, he didn't chase after it. Just watched it bounce down the sidewalk.

His bark didn't even sound the same. It sounded like whining, not barking.

"Why is Rusty so weird?" Emma asked. "He won't even let me pet him."

"He had a scare," Mom said. "It will take him a while to get over it."

"At least we got him back," I said. "Our good luck doesn't stop."

The next day, Dad picked Emma and me up at school. He usually asked us a lot of questions about our day. But today he didn't say a word. He kept his lips pressed tightly together. His eyes looked watery, as if he was about to cry.

"Dad, is anything wrong?" I asked. "You look really sad."

He sighed. "I might as well tell you. You will hear it soon enough."

"What?" I cried. "What is wrong?"

He kept his eyes straight on the road. He didn't look at me.

"I lost my job today," he said.

"Oh noooo!" Emma cried from the back seat. "You were fired?"

Dad nodded and sighed again. "I worked there ten years. And they let me go—just like that."

Emma and I were silent for a while. Finally, I said, "You know we're the Lucky family. You know we have good luck. You'll find a new job right away, Dad."

I saw a teardrop slide down his cheek. He didn't say anything. Just kept his eyes straight ahead on the road.

A few mornings later, Dad dressed up in a suit and tie. "I have a good job interview this morning," he said at breakfast. "I think I can wow them. I think I can get a great new job."

Emma and I slapped Dad high-fives. Mom hugged him. He pulled open the front door. But he didn't leave.

"Oh, wow." He shook his head. "Oh, wow." His mouth dropped open. He stared down to the street.

"Dad—?" I started.

"Our car has been stolen," he said. "I'm going to miss the job interview."

To my surprise, Emma grabbed me by the arms. She shook me hard. "Your charm doesn't work, Chuck!" she screamed. "Don't you see? We're not lucky! We're not lucky at all!"

On Saturday morning, I found the black velvet bag on the floor near the trash cans. The silvery shamrock was inside it. I knew that Dad had taken it off because it didn't work. It brought us only bad luck.

I showed it to Emma. "I'm going to take it back to that store and tell the old guy Mr. Fogg his charm is no good," I said.

"Do you think he'll give your money back?" she asked.

"It was free," I told her. "He gave it to me as a gift. But I want to tell him it doesn't work. He said everything in his store is real, and that's not true."

"Can I come with you?" Emma asked. "Please please please."

I shrugged. "I guess." Actually, I was happy to have her come with me. I really didn't want to do it alone.

Mom and Dad were shopping for groceries. I left them a note on the kitchen table. Then I tucked the black velvet bag into my jeans pocket, and Emma and I took the bus into town.

We stopped in front of the store. Emma read the sign: ODD THINGS. She studied all the strange creatures and objects in the front window. "Creepy," she said, shivering. "Are you sure you want to go back inside there?"

I pulled the bag from my pocket. "We have to return it," I said. I tugged open the glass door and we stepped inside.

Emma shivered again. "It's c-cold in here," she stammered. "And why is it so dark?"

"Bright lights hurt my eyes," a croaky voice said.

Mr. Fogg stood behind the counter. "How can I help you?"

I placed the bag in front of him on the counter. "I have to return the lucky charm," I said. "It didn't work."

He squinted down at it. "Didn't work?"

"No," Emma chimed in. "Ever since Chuck got it, we've had nothing but bad luck."

"I don't believe that," Mr. Fogg said.

"It's true," I said. "Nothing but bad luck. I was hit by a car, and our house burned down, and our dog ran away, and I hammered a nail through my hand, and my dad lost his job, and our car was stolen."

The old man swallowed loudly. He blinked several times. "Hmmmm. Bad luck. Very bad luck," he muttered.

He reached into the bag and slid the shamrock out. "Let me take a look."

He held it up close to his face. He studied one side, then the other. His bright blue eyes shone on the metal shamrock until it appeared to glow.

Then he lowered it to the counter. "Did anyone drop this charm?" he asked. "Did anyone drop it on the floor or crash it against something?"

I thought hard. "Well . . . Emma dropped it once. Onto the floor in my hospital room."

"It was an accident," Emma said.

"I thought so," Mr. Fogg said. "You see, one of the letters on the back fell off. Where it said *Lucky Charm.*"

"Huh? I don't understand," I said.

He held the back of the charm up to Emma and me. "See?" he said. "The letter *C* came off."

I read the stenciled words on the charm: *Lucky harm.*
Lucky HARM?

"That's why you had all the bad luck," Mr. Fogg said.

I stared at the back of the shamrock for a long time, reading the words over and over. "I still need to return it," I said.

He shut his eyes. The blue light disappeared. "You can't return it," he whispered. "It's very bad luck to return it."

"But it's bad luck to *keep* it," Emma said.

"It can't be returned. I'm sorry." He dropped it into the bag and slid the bag across the countertop at me. "You must keep it, or your luck will be even worse."

I didn't know what to do. I gazed at Emma and she gazed back at me. She didn't know what to do, either.

"Okay," I murmured finally. I grabbed the bag, turned, and started to the door.

I heard his cane tapping the floor as Mr. Fogg disappeared to the back of the store. When he was out of sight, I raised the bag and tossed it onto a high shelf. Then Emma and I hurried out of the store as fast as we could.

We trotted down the sidewalk, and we both started to laugh. "I'm so glad we got rid of that thing," Emma said.

And then she fell down an open manhole.

"Nooooo!" I cried.

I leaped forward and grabbed her around the waist as she started to sink into the hole. I held on tight and struggled to hoist her out.

"I've got you!" I shouted. "I've got you!"

I swung her back onto the sidewalk. She caught her balance, and a smile spread over her face. She was perfectly fine.

"From now on," I said, "we make our *own* luck!"

LOST AND FOUND

I grew up in Columbus, Ohio. Every school year our class would take a field trip to the Columbus Zoo. It's a wonderful zoo that seems to go on for miles, sprawled along the Olentangy River.

One year when I was in third or fourth grade, I wandered away from my friends and found myself in the giraffe house. I don't know why I found them so interesting. But I stared up at the giraffes for a long time, and they stared back at me.

It was like I was in a trance. When I finally walked back outside, I couldn't find my class. I gazed all around. I made my way to the Jungle area. No sign of them. I checked the penguin house. Then the polar bear exhibit.

The sun had started to go down. I heard animals roaring in the distance.

We didn't have cell phones back then. How would I ever find my friends? I was lost, lost in the zoo.

I remembered that frightening *lost* feeling when I wrote this story.

I WAS EXCITED AND I KNEW MY FRIEND AUDRA JOHNSON WAS
excited, too. We both love animals and, for us, the sixth-grade trip to the Mid-Town Zoo was the best school day of the year.

The zoo is only about half an hour out of town. But our parents were always too busy to take us. We were both dying to see the new African Plains area. The ads on TV said it was like going on a real safari.

Audra and I watched the videos of the African Plains exhibit on YouTube. But it definitely wasn't the same as being there. I mean, can you imagine breathing the same air as lions and gazelles and wildebeests?

"Rosie, maybe we can become vets and work in a zoo," Audra said after we watched the videos for a fourth time. "Wouldn't that be awesome?"

"Awesome," I agreed. See? We really are animal freaks.

We planned to record our zoo trip and edit our videos together into a long video journal. So when our sixth-grade teacher, Mr. Glick, began describing the big day, we both sat on the edge of our chairs, listening eagerly.

But before Mr. Glick even got started, Marty Blasingame had his hand up and started to complain about how he's allergic to animal dander, whatever that is. And what could Mr. Glick do about it?

You can stay on the bus, creepoid, I thought. *Or why don't you stay home and hide under the bed?*

I know that's not kind. Maybe you can tell I'm not a Marty Blasingame fan.

Marty has ruined just about every school trip we ever had. He even messed up the spring picnic by being allergic to fresh air or something. I'm not sure why, but his head swelled up like a pumpkin. He sure made a big deal about it.

Mr. Glick told him he should take an antihistamine the morning of the trip. Marty nodded, but I knew that wouldn't be the end of it.

Mr. Glick told us to save our questions till the end of his talk. Then he started to tell us what he had planned for the day, and he pretty much ruined the whole thing.

"We'll start the day with a lecture by one of the zoo's top workers," he said. "She'll be telling us about endangered species and what we can do to help preserve them."

Endangered species?

I heard Audra groan. I didn't groan, but I rolled my eyes.

We already know about endangered species. We don't want to sit through a long, boring lecture. We want to see the animals close-up.

Marty Blasingame had his hand up again. "Will the talk be indoors or outdoors?" he asked. "If it's indoors, I'm allergic to certain animal smells."

I didn't listen to Mr. Glick's answer. Audra and I were looking at each other across the room. I knew we were both thinking the same thing. *Maybe we can skip the lecture and go out on our own.*

Two days later, on the school bus taking us to the zoo, Audra and I sat in back. We made a list of the animals we wanted to capture on video.

Mr. Glick stood up at the front of the bus. He's very tall, so he took his cap off and ducked his head beneath the bus ceiling. "I have some good news," he said.

"Uh-oh," I muttered to Audra. We both knew the news was probably not great.

"We're in luck," Mr. Glick said. He looked down at the stack of papers in his hand. "Elena Fong, the assistant zookeeper, is also going to give a talk this morning. She's going to tell us what it's like to work in a zoo."

Two lectures?

This time, Audra and I both groaned.

"Does that leave any time to see animals?" I asked him.

But he turned and dropped back into his seat behind the driver. He didn't hear me.

"Well, now we have no choice, Rosie," Audra said in a low voice just above a whisper. "*No way* we're sitting through two lectures."

"We'll ditch the class and head to the African Plains," I whispered back.

Marty Blasingame turned in his seat in front of us. He sniffed the air and stared at Audra. "What's that smell?" he asked. "What are you eating?"

"It's a beef jerky stick," Audra said. She raised it toward him. "I'm addicted. Want one?"

Marty made a disgusted face. "Get that away. I'm allergic to jerky. It gives me a bad rash," he said.

Big surprise.

Audra turned to me. "I loaded my pockets with them in case we get hungry," she said.

A short while later, the bus squealed to a stop. I stared out the window at the tall gates and the big sign shaped like a camel with the words WELCOME TO MID-TOWN ZOO.

Since Audra and I were sitting at the very back, we stepped off the bus last. My heart started to beat a little faster as I gazed around the front gates. Yes, I was excited to be there. But I also felt tense knowing what Audra and I planned to do.

What if we get caught?

"Don't think about it," Audra said, as if she could read my mind. She held me back with one arm. "Wait."

We watched the others follow Mr. Glick to the entrance turnstiles. "Okay," Audra whispered.

No one was watching. We both took off, running toward the side of the iron fence. My shoes pounded the parking lot pavement. Would we really get away with this?

"Hey! Come back!"

"Oh noo!" I moaned. That was Mr. Glick's shout.

I froze. My breath stuck in my throat.

We were caught.

Struggling to breathe, I spun around. And saw Mr. Glick chasing after his papers. The papers sailed across the pavement, blown by the wind.

Audra laughed. "He wasn't shouting at us," she said. "He was shouting at his papers." She gave me a shove. "Let's go!"

We darted around the side of the tall fence and kept running. No one could see us now. I stopped at a narrow gap in the fence, breathing hard.

I turned sideways and slipped through the opening. Audra caught her jeans on the jagged metal. I grabbed her hands and pulled her through.

We were in the zoo!

We took a moment to catch our breath. I gazed around. A group of low buildings stretched just beyond a wide, grassy square. I recognized the penguin house at the far end.

The tall building beside it was a creepy place. It had all the nocturnal animals, so it was completely dark inside.

Food and ice cream stands lined the path to the buildings. They were empty, gates pulled closed over their fronts.

"Where is everyone?" Audra asked. "We're the only ones here."

"It's Tuesday morning," I said. "Kids are all in school. People are at work." I pumped my fists in the air. "It's all ours! The zoo is all ours!"

We didn't waste time. We followed the signs toward the African Plains. The path led through a thick clump of tall, leafy trees. I could hear the chittering of animals over our heads. Were there monkeys in the trees?

I gazed up, but leaves blocked the sunlight. It was too dark to see anything.

We came out of the trees and followed the path through some tall grass and then a clump of evergreen bushes. Large black birds with very wide wings soared high in the blue sky. Were they hawks?

"I can't believe we're going to have the African Plains all to ourselves!" Audra exclaimed.

"This is way cool," I agreed. "Too bad we're missing those *interesting* lectures!" We both laughed.

We came to the entrance of the African Plains. A white ticket booth stood beside two turnstiles. The ticket booth was closed. We ducked under the turnstiles. We were in!

We followed the dirt path up a sloping hill. Low shrubs covered the ground till we got to the top of the hill. They gave way to skinny, brown reeds waving from side to side in the breeze.

"Rosie, we don't have to stay on the path," Audra said. "Who is going to make us?"

I turned. "Let's cut through these reeds."

The tall reeds brushed against us as we made our own path. Where were we headed? I didn't know. For a brief second it flashed into my mind that it wouldn't be good to get lost here.

But whoever got lost in a zoo?

"Oh, wow! Look!" Audra cried, pointing.

"I see them," I said.

The reeds ended at a low brick wall. On the other side of the wall stretched a wide, grassy lawn.

Audra and I stood open-mouthed, staring at a herd of gazelles around the lawn. A dozen of them? Two dozen?

They were spread out. Some stood grazing on the grass. Others were sprawled on the ground, sunbathing, I guess. Two little gazelles were huddled around their mother.

"This is awesome!" I said.

A few of the creatures raised their heads and turned toward us. But they didn't seem startled or worried. "It's so quiet. They're chilling," I said. "It's like their day off."

"Think we can go closer?" Audra asked.

We took a few steps toward them. A few more gazelles raised their heads. They were definitely watching us now.

"Our video," Audra said. "We have to start recording—" She stopped short.

We both groaned.

Our backpacks. We'd left them under our seats on the school bus with our phones in them.

Audra pressed her hands to her cheeks. "I can't believe we didn't bring our phones."

I shook my head. "What was I thinking? I was so tense about sneaking away from the others . . ."

We stared at each other for a long moment.

Finally, I said, "Oh, well. We can have an awesome day without doing the video. And think of the good news."

Audra rolled her eyes. "What good news?"

"We missed the two lectures."

That made us both laugh again. And I guess maybe we laughed a little too loud. The gazelles on the ground suddenly climbed to their feet. And now they were alert and standing stiffly—and all staring straight ahead at us, their heads raised, sniffing the air.

"No," I muttered. "Oh no." A heavy feeling of dread rolled down my body. And it froze me in place as the gazelles moved together, pawed the ground—and came charging at us.

Heads lowered, they stampeded. Their hooves thudded loudly over the grass. Grunting and bleating, they thundered toward us.

"Run!" Audra cried, grabbing my hand and pulling me out of my shock.

We both spun around and took off, the *thud* of the hooves drumming in our ears. The angry animal cries roaring over the air.

We jumped over the low brick wall and kept running.

Would the gazelles stop at the wall? Or would they keep coming?

I didn't turn back to find out.

The pounding hoofbeats sounded so close. The only thing louder was the beating of my heart.

We raced through tall grass. My chest felt about to burst. I'd never run that fast. The grass ended at a round pond covered in some kind of green scummy stuff. We turned and followed the shoreline, our shoes sinking in soft mud.

A patch of prickly bushes led to a line of tall trees. "I . . . I think we can stop," I choked out. "I don't hear them anymore."

My throat ached and my left side throbbed with pain.

We stood there panting, bent over, hands on our knees.

The sun drifted behind clouds, and long shadows spread over the ground. The air grew cooler.

I finally began to breathe normally. "We outran them," I said. "I think they would have stampeded right over us."

"But . . . where are we?" Audra said. She gazed around in a circle. Nothing but trees and long grass and weeds.

"I don't see any zoo signs," I said. "I guess we went too far from the paths."

Audra sighed. "There's no one else here," she said softly. "And no sunlight, so we can't tell what direction we're facing."

I tried to fight it. But that feeling of dread rolled down over me like a cold chill. "Are we—are we lost?" I stammered.

Audra swallowed. "I can't believe we're lost, and we don't have our phones."

Silence for a long moment. A dozen thoughts raced through my mind. All of them frightening. "I guess we should keep walking," I said finally. "We'll come to a path or something eventually, don't you think?"

"I don't know," Audra said. "I don't want to be the brave one, Rosie. I think you have to be the brave one."

"I don't feel like the brave one," I replied. Then another frightening thought: "You don't think they'll leave without us, do you?"

"Of course not," Audra replied. "They'll search till they find us. But Mr. Glick won't be happy. We'll be in major trouble."

"If we tell him we were caught in a gazelle stampede . . ." I started.

"That won't help," Audra said. "Let's keep walking."

We made our way through the trees. I kept looking up, hoping the sun would come back. Our shoes rattled the carpet of dead leaves on the ground. An animal scurried over my feet. I didn't know what it was.

A few minutes later, we came to the swampy pond again. "Uh-oh, Rosie," Audra murmured. "I think we're walking in circles."

I pointed to the left. "Let's try that direction." Audra had her head down. "Are you scared?" I asked.

"Not scared," she said in a quiet voice. "Just disappointed. We had such a nice plan."

"Well, at least we'll have a story to tell," I said, trying to keep it cheerful.

Audra and I walked in silence for another ten minutes or so. We climbed a low, sloping hill, then followed the patchy grass down the other side.

"Whoa." I uttered a cry of surprise as we walked up to a chain-wire fence. "There's a sign."

We stepped closer. The sign had black block letters on it. It read: DANGER. ENDANGERED.

"What does that mean?" Audra asked. "What animals do they keep here?"

"Might as well find out," I said. I held the fence down so she could climb over it. Then she did the same for me.

We followed a path through evergreen shrubs that reached high over our heads. The path kept twisting and turning like a maze.

When we finally came out the other end, we both stared in amazement.

Little houses. Dozens of small white houses with slanty red roofs. Not much bigger than doghouses. Lined up in several rows.

"A whole village of little cottages," I murmured. "Do they keep animals here?"

Audra opened her mouth to answer. But she stopped when a door opened on the nearest cottage—and a little man stepped out.

I grabbed her arm. I blinked several times, trying to clear my eyes. I *had* to be seeing things.

But no. He was real. He was about two feet tall, dressed in red tights and a green sweater. He had a wrinkled old man's face and a short white beard and wore a pointy red cap, like Santa's elves wear.

He didn't see us. He turned and walked the other way. He walked slowly, wobbling from side to side. Another bearded little man, dressed in the same red and green colors, stepped out to greet him. They began chattering at each other in high chipmunk voices.

"This . . . isn't real," I whispered to Audra.

She squinted at the two tiny men. "They look exactly like the lawn gnomes on my grandpa's front lawn," she said.

Yes. She was right. Lawn gnomes. My uncle Norman has two of them in his yard. And about a year ago, I watched a scary movie about lawn gnomes on Netflix.

I held on to Audra's arm as we stared in amazement. Another cottage door swung open and two tiny women stepped out. They wore long green dresses and pointy red caps over their white hair. One of them leaned on a cane as she walked.

"Maybe we shouldn't be seeing this," I whispered. Audra and I took a step back.

Then we both screamed as something heavy crashed over us.

We both fell to our knees and hit the ground hard. A net. A thick rope net covered us and held us down.

I screamed again and tried to shove the net off. "Too heavy!" I groaned.

Audra and I both struggled with it. But we were trapped. Trapped on our knees. And when I looked up, we were surrounded by the little men and women.

They stared through the net at us, wide-eyed and

open-mouthed. Some of the men rubbed their beards as they watched us. Three women hung back, whispering to one another. They all looked as surprised as we were.

"Let us go!" I screamed. "Let us out!"

They muttered to themselves. Leaning on his cane, a very old-looking man with gray, tired eyes hobbled close to us. "I'm Olaf the Elder," he said. "How did you find us?" His voice was scratchy, squeaky like a cartoon voice. "How?"

"We . . . we were lost . . . ," I started.

"No one has found our village before," he said. His pale eyes slid from Audra to me. "Did you come for pebbles?"

"Huh? Pebbles?" I said. "No. We don't want pebbles. We don't want anything. We just want to go back to our class."

"Let us out!" Audra said. "We don't want anything. And we're not going to hurt you."

To my surprise, the old man waved an arm. Several of the little people stepped forward. They formed a line around the net and tugged it off us.

Audra and I climbed to our feet and brushed off our jeans. They formed a tight circle around us, studying us as if we were exotic zoo animals.

"Who are you?" I demanded. "Please tell us. Do you live here?"

36

I know it was a dumb question. But I was crazed. I kept thinking I was dreaming.

"Of course we live here," Olaf the Elder answered with a sneer. "We're zoo gnomes. So we live in the zoo."

I squinted at him, my mind spinning. "Zoo gnomes?"

"Don't fret that you don't know us," he said in his squeaky voice. "We have our village here because we don't want to be found."

A younger gnome in a green sweater and tights and bright white boots stomped forward. "I'm Olaf the Younger. We want to live our lives without staring eyes," he said. "We want to be left alone."

"S-sorry," I stammered. "We didn't know—"

"Most people don't believe in us," the old gnome said. "We like to keep it that way. We feel safe here. No one ever visits this part of the zoo."

I opened my mouth to reply to him, but I didn't know what to say.

"How did you find us? Where did you come from?" Olaf the Younger demanded.

"We got lost," Audra told him. "We were running from some gazelles and got turned around."

That started the gnomes all chattering at once.

"Can you tell us how to get back to the zoo entrance?" I asked.

I waited, but no one answered my question.

A woman with straight white hair down almost to her knees stepped forward. She held a white mouse in one hand and was petting its back. She shook her head. "We thought we were safe," she murmured.

"Don't worry," I said. "We won't tell anyone."

"No, you won't," the old gnome replied.

I didn't like the sound of that. Was it some kind of threat? His pale eyes had suddenly gone cold. The others grew silent.

Audra turned and whispered to me, "If only we had our phones. This would be an amazing video."

"I just want to get back," I whispered.

"What do you do here in the middle of nowhere?" Audra asked them. "How do you live?"

The woman pointed to a high pile of gray rocks at the other end of the village. "We grind rocks into pebbles," she said.

I couldn't hide my surprise. "Rocks into pebbles? Why?"

The old gnome frowned at me. "Why question it? We've been doing it for hundreds of years. I'm one hundred and five, and I've been pounding pebbles for at least a hundred years."

He gave a signal, and the gnomes behind us began to move forward. It took me a few seconds to realize they were forcing us to move, forcing us to the middle of the village.

We walked past several of the small red-roofed cottages. At the side of one of them, two gnomes wearing long white aprons stood over a fire. I gasped when I realized they were roasting two chipmunks on a spit.

"We're meat eaters," Olaf the Younger said. He reached up and pinched my arm. "You're kinda bony."

I pulled my arm away. He was starting to scare me. "Please. Can you point the way to the front of the zoo?" I asked. "We have to get back to our class."

"We can't let you leave," Olaf the Elder said. "You've seen us."

He gave another signal. I heard a clatter all around us. Several gnomes raised crossbows and aimed them at us.

"Whoa. Wait!" I cried. "We won't tell anyone about you! We promise!"

I saw the look of fear on Audra's face. She grabbed my hand and tugged me forward. Without saying a word, we took off. We burst right through the line of gnomes, sending them sprawling to their backs on the grass.

Ducking our heads, we ran toward the fence.

"Oww!" I cried out as something pinched my arm. "Oww!" Again. A little arrow stuck in my shoulder.

A *ping ping ping* sound rang in my ears as the gnomes shot off their crossbows, and arrows rained over us.

Audra and I stopped. We tugged arrows from our arms and backs. "Ouch. Ouch. Ouch."

We had no choice. We raised our hands in surrender.

The armed gnomes marched us back to Olaf the Elder.

I rubbed the stinging pain from my arms. "You're really not going to let us go? What are you going to do with us?" I asked.

"We're going to put you in our Lost and Found," he replied. "Maybe someone will claim you."

"But we're not lost!" I cried.

"And no one knows you gnomes are here!" Audra added. "No one will come to claim us."

"We'll keep you in the Lost and Found for three weeks," the old gnome said.

I made a gulping sound. "Then what?" I said.

"Then we'll probably eat you," he replied. "You're bony, but you'll be a nice break from chipmunks."

"But—but—" I sputtered. "You don't want to eat us. We're *humans*—like you!"

Olaf the Elder chuckled into his beard. "We're not humans. We're gnomes. We've been eating people for hundreds of years."

The armed gnomes led us to a fenced-in pen. A sign on the front read: LOST AND FOUND. They pulled open the gate and began to push us inside.

But Audra stopped and spun around. "Oh, wait. We forgot," she said. "We have gifts for you."

Olaf the Elder stepped forward and gazed at us suspiciously. "Gifts?"

I stared at Audra. *Gifts? What is she talking about?*

I watched as Audra reached both hands into her jeans pockets. What was she pulling out? Beef jerky! Five or six sticks of beef jerky!

"Meat!" she cried. And tossed them on the ground in front of the surprised gnomes.

The gnomes uttered frantic cries—and dove for the jerky sticks.

We didn't hesitate. We took off again. Lowered our heads and ran right through the scrambling gnomes. We darted past cottages and onto the grassy field.

Little arrows zinged by our heads. We kept low and ran faster than we'd ever run. We leaped over the wire fence with the sign that read: DANGER. ENDANGERED.

The arrows were flying wildly now, not even close. I glanced back. We had left the gnomes far behind.

But we didn't slow down. We ran till we found a path. And we followed it to a sign with a painted arrow and the words ZOO ENTRANCE.

We were breathing hard, drenched in sweat when we reached the front gate. I shut my eyes and waited for my sides to stop aching and my breathing to slow to normal.

Then I gazed all around. "Audra—where's our class?"

Her mouth dropped open. "I don't see anyone. They . . . they wouldn't leave without us."

I opened my mouth to reply but stopped when I heard a shout. I turned to the voice—and saw Mr. Glick and everyone else on the other side of the iron fence.

"You two are in deep doo-doo!" Marty Blasingame shouted. A lot of kids laughed.

Audra and I darted to the fence. I moved close to Mr. Glick. "How come you're still in the parking lot?" I asked through the fence.

"There was a power shortage," he replied. "The zoo has been closed since early this morning. No one has been allowed in."

Marty Blasingame sneezed. "I told you, I'm allergic to waiting in a parking lot for so long."

"Go sit in the bus," Mr. Glick snapped at him. He turned back to Audra and me. "We've all been frantic waiting for you. You'd better have a good story, or you are both in very big trouble."

"We do have a good story," Audra said.

"We ran from a gazelle stampede. And then we were kidnapped by zoo gnomes," I told him. "They were going to keep us prisoner in their Lost and Found and then eat us."

Mr. Glick groaned and rolled his eyes. "Is that the best

you can do?" He shook his head. "Do you honestly believe anyone would believe a story like that?"

"It's true! It's true!" we both cried.

The teacher stared from Audra to me. "If you don't tell me the truth, I'm afraid you'll have to be suspended from school."

"Show us the photos!" Marty Blasingame cried. "You can prove it. Easy. Show us the photos you took."

"We—we left our phones on the bus," I stammered. "We don't have any photos."

Mr. Glick stared at us a while longer without saying anything. Finally, he waved a hand. "Climb over the fence. Come out here to the parking lot. We have to go back to school. I'm so sorry. But you've left me no choice but to report this to the principal and your parents."

I sighed and led the way out of the zoo and onto the school bus. Audra and I took our seats in the back row. We didn't talk. We didn't even look at each other.

I kept thinking about my mom and dad, how unhappy they'd be when they got the call from the school. *They'll be so angry.*

And there was no way to prove our story. No way . . .

Marty Blasingame turned around and laughed in the seat in front of us. "Zoo gnomes," he said. "Good one. You two must have been dreaming."

I turned to Audra. "Maybe we *were* dreaming," I murmured.

Marty slapped his baseball cap. "If you two discovered zoo gnomes, I'll eat this cap."

"Give us a break, Marty," Audra said. "We know we're in major trouble."

"Oh." I let out a cry as the bus rocked to a sudden stop. My elbow bumped the arm of my seat. I let out another cry as I felt a sharp pain in my shoulder.

I reached my hand to rub away the pain—and pulled something from my shoulder.

A tiny arrow.

I held it up to Audra. A grin spread across her face.

Then I reached across the seatback and pulled off Marty's baseball cap. I pushed it in front of his face. "Hope you're not allergic," I said. "Start chewing."

MIND BLOWERS

I started writing in fourth grade when I was nine years old. I loved staying in my room and typing story after story. I guess I was a weird kid.

I was never any good at sports. When I played softball with my friends after school, I grounded out from short to first every time I came up to bat. I never got a hit.

When we were choosing up teams in gym class, I was always the *last* to be chosen. The captains would fight over who had to take me.

Sometimes I wondered what it would be like to be good at sports like other kids. What if I could become one of those sports-star kids just for a day?

That's where the idea for this story came from.

"I'M SORRY THOSE PAJAMAS I BOUGHT ARE TOO BIG FOR YOU, Skippy," Aunt Judith said. "I can return them for a smaller size."

I pulled them out of her hands. "No. No problem. I'll grow into them. Mom says I'm going to have a growth spurt any day now."

She took a sip from her coffee mug. "Well, tell me. How is third grade treating you?"

I groaned and gritted my teeth. "Aunt Judith, I'm not in third grade," I said. "I'm in *sixth* grade."

Her cheeks turned pink. She blinked a few times. "I'm sorry, Skippy—" she started.

"Know what the kids in my class call me?" I said. "Not Skippy. They call me Shrimpy."

My aunt made a *tsk-tsk* sound. "That's not nice."

"Tell me about it," I said. I sighed. "I'm so tired of being the smallest kid in my class."

"Everyone grows at their own rate of speed," Mom said. She says it a lot. I don't even know what it means.

Later, I met my friend Lucas. We tossed a tennis ball back and forth in his backyard until it got boring. "What do you want to do?" he asked. "It's a nice day. Why don't we head over to the playground and see who is hanging there?"

"I don't think so," I said. "I've been staying away from the playground ever since last week."

"Huh?" He squinted at me. "What happened last week?"

"Harvey Meadows and his pals grabbed me and had a contest to see who could toss me the farthest."

"You're joking," Lucas said.

"No joke. They called it a Shrimpy Toss. Harvey tossed me eight feet. I'm still bruised."

"Oh, wow." Lucas shook his head. "Harvey is a bully. Did you tell anyone about it?"

"I was afraid to," I replied. "Harvey is so big. If he sat on me, he'd crush me."

Poochy barked at us from the kitchen window. He hates being separated from me.

"Want to take Poochy to the playground?" Lucas asked.

I shook my head. "Honestly, I'm afraid to walk Poochy. He's so big, I'm afraid he'll pick me up and bury me in the sand."

Lucas laughed. "Skippy, you should do a comedy act about being small."

"It isn't funny," I muttered.

That night, Dad brought home a big fried chicken bucket, and we were sitting around the kitchen table having dinner. Poochy huddled under the table, hoping someone would drop some chicken.

Mom passed the gravy and I let it ooze over my mashed potatoes. "You have a big twelfth birthday coming up, Skip," she said. "What do you want for your birthday?"

I didn't have to think about it. "I want to be six inches taller," I said.

Dad lowered the drumstick from his mouth. "Okay," he said. "Done. We can do that." He had a strange grin on his face.

"Huh? What are you talking about?" I said.

His grin grew wider. "You'll see," he said.

The morning of my birthday, we all piled into the car. Poochy, too. My parents said they had an awesome surprise for me. I begged them to tell me what it was, but they both zipped their fingers over their lips.

We drove through town and stopped at a long, low building a few miles into the country. The building looked like a big concrete slab. I noticed right away that it had no windows.

We climbed out of the car. Mom and Dad planned to leave Poochy. But he started barking, so Dad grabbed his leash and brought him with us.

We followed the path to the front entrance, a narrow gray door the same color as the building. I saw a sign beside the door. In bold black letters, it read: MIND BLOWERS.

I stopped and squinted at the sign. Poochy bumped into me and nearly knocked me over. "What does that mean?" I demanded. "What is this place?"

"You'll see," Mom said.

Dad pulled open the door. "It's your birthday surprise," he said. He had that grin on his face again. Like he was bursting to tell me what was going on.

We stepped into a long white reception room. Brown leather chairs lined one wall. At the far end, a woman saw us and stood up from behind a large metal desk.

She put a smile on her face and came walking toward us. Her heels clicked loudly on the hard floor. She was young, younger than my parents, and had wavy brown hair down to her shoulders, dark eyes that seemed to lock on me, and purple lipstick that glowed under the bright ceiling lights.

She kept her hands in the pockets of her white lab coat. As she came closer, I read the brass name tag on her shirt collar: *Dr. Allison Ripple*. "You must be Skippy," she said, and her smile grew wider.

"I'm Dr. Ripple." She motioned with both hands for us to take seats. Poochy ducked under one of the chairs and began sniffing the wall.

"What is your dog's name?" she asked me.

"Poochy," I said.

"Clever," she replied. *Is she making a joke?*

I sat down between Mom and Dad. "What is this place?" I asked.

She narrowed her eyes at me. "Didn't your parents tell you?"

"It's a surprise," Mom said.

Dr. Ripple nodded. "Well, I think it will be a nice surprise for you, Skippy," she said. "We're going to make your birthday wish come true."

I stared back at her. I didn't know what to say.

She pulled a chair out and spun it around to face us. She sat down and clasped her hands in front of her. "Your parents told me you would like to change," she said. "Well, I'm going to give you a change you won't believe."

"Ch-change?" I stammered. I still didn't know what to say.

"Let me explain," she said. "Here at Mind Blowers, we blow your mind."

I laughed. "You *what*?"

"We blow your mind into another person's body," she continued. "You get to live inside someone else's body—and *be* that person for twenty-four hours. And they get to be you."

My jaw dropped open. "Whoooaa . . ." *This has to be a joke, right?*

"I know it sounds unreal," Dr. Ripple said. "But it's your mind in another body for a whole day. It's like taking a vacation from your body."

Dad slapped me on the back. "I knew you'd like this, Skip," he said. "We've seen photos of the other kid. Wait till you see him."

"We've talked to his parents, too," Mom added. "They're as excited as we are."

Dr. Ripple jumped to her feet and motioned us up. "Follow me. Hardy is already waiting in the Mind-Blowing Chamber."

She led us through double doors, into a large chamber the size of a gym. The walls were mirrors on all four sides. In the middle of the floor, I saw a curtained booth. Like a long tent.

A boy about my age stood at one end of the booth. His parents stood beside him. Our shoes clattered on the hardwood floor as we walked toward them.

I kept my eyes on him. He was big, at least a foot taller than me. He had broad shoulders and powerful-looking arms bulging from his T-shirt. Even his head was bigger than mine!

Hardy had curly red hair and a face full of freckles. His green eyes studied me just as I was studying him.

His parents were big, too. His dad had a shiny bald head, but his mom had the same curly red hair and freckles as Hardy.

"Hardy Harper, meet Skippy Simon," Dr. Ripple said.

"Hey," I said. We nodded to each other.

Mom and Dad introduced themselves to the Harpers. Dad made a joke. He said, "I guess *we'll* be getting a vacation from our kids, too." He laughed but no one else did.

"This is an exciting opportunity for you boys," Dr. Ripple said. "You get to lead each other's life for twenty-four hours."

"This will be so much fun!" Mrs. Harper gushed. "Skippy, you'll get to play in Hardy's big soccer game this afternoon."

I blinked. "Soccer game?"

"Do you like cheeseburgers?" Hardy's dad asked me. "That's Hardy's favorite. I'm grilling cheeseburgers tonight for dinner."

"I work out a lot," Hardy said, "and I play all sports. Soccer is my best sport. But I'm pretty good at lacrosse and tennis and wrestling, and I have a lot of swimming trophies." He squinted at me. "What do *you* like to do?"

"Well . . ." I had to think. "I like to read *manga* comics. I have a big collection. And I like to play video games online with kids."

"Awesome," Hardy replied. "I need a break."

Poochy barked and tried to pull away from Dad. The big dog wanted to check out the curtained booth. Dad used both hands on the leash to tug him back.

"I think we should get started," Dr. Ripple said. "We don't want the equipment to overheat." She pointed to one end of the booth. "Skippy, why don't you go in that side? And, Hardy, you enter on the other side."

I hesitated. I had a sudden heavy feeling of fear in the pit of my stomach. "Are you sure this is safe?"

Dr. Ripple nodded. "We've blown dozens of minds, Skippy. Everyone has always had fun."

"You'll be big and strong for a whole day," Dad said. "You got your birthday wish."

"Th-thanks," I stammered. I stepped into the booth.

Poochy started to bark. He doesn't like to be separated from me.

I waited for my eyes to adjust to the dim light, and then I gazed around. I saw a low wooden stool in front of a tall metal control panel with flashing white lights. A round red button poked out from the panel. A pair of headphones dangled over the wooden stool.

"Sit down, boys, and put on the headphones." Dr. Ripple's voice came from a speaker above my head.

I dropped onto the stool and pulled the headphones over my ears. I heard a low hum . . . and then Dr. Ripple's voice. "This is very easy," she said. "It's simple and painless and amazingly quick. Are you boys nervous?"

We both called out no. I was kind of lying. My throat felt dry and tight, and I clasped my hands on my lap to keep them from shaking.

"When the red button lights up, just push it," she instructed. "That's all you have to do, and your minds will be blown into each other's body."

I realized I was holding my breath. I let it out in a long whoosh and stared at the button in front of me. The control panel began to hum louder. The hum became a steady buzz.

I gasped when the button lit up red. And I pushed it.

A powerful burst of wind blasted my back. The force of it shoved me off the stool onto my knees. Bright lights swirled around me.

The lights grew brighter and brighter, and the roar of wind filled my ears. I tugged off the headphones, trying to make the deafening roar stop. But the roar was inside my head. I shut my eyes and gritted my teeth.

Was my head about to *explode*?

"Oh." I uttered a soft cry of surprise as it all stopped. I blinked, waiting for the blinding light to fade from my eyes. Leaning on the wooden stool, I climbed shakily to my feet. I took a few unsteady steps.

"Whoa." Everything felt different. My legs were heavier. My shoes banged the floor. I felt awkward, as if I'd never walked before.

I made my way out of the curtained booth—and stopped. I saw myself immediately in the mirrored wall.

I was Hardy.

My breath caught in my throat. I nearly choked. I stared in disbelief at my red hair, my big head, my powerful arms, my broad chest, my long legs!

I turned away from the mirror and saw myself walk out from the other side of the booth. I mean, I saw my *body* walk out. My body with Hardy's mind inside.

He stopped in shock, just as I had, and stared at himself in the mirror.

Mr. and Mrs. Harper went running over to him. "How is it?" his mom cried.

He moved his shoulders around and stretched his arms. "It's a little cramped in here," he said.

Dr. Ripple laughed. "You'll have to get used to a smaller body, Hardy. How does it feel to be so much lighter?"

"Weird," he answered.

My parents stood open-mouthed, staring at me. Poochy let out a low growl and backed up between them, watching me suspiciously.

I wasn't used to the weight. I clomped heavily over to them. "It worked," I told them. "It's me. Skippy. I'm inside Hardy."

Dad squeezed my shoulder. "Happy birthday, son," he said.

Mom brushed back my red hair with one hand. "Enjoy!" she said.

"Thank you," I said. "This is going to be the best vacation I ever had. A vacation from my body!"

"Check the time, everyone," Dr. Ripple said. "You must be back here exactly twenty-four hours from now so you can switch back."

Mr. Harper checked his phone. He motioned to me. "We've got to scoot. You don't want to be late for your soccer game. They're all counting on you, Hardy."

And that's exactly what the soccer coach said to me when we arrived at the game. Players from both teams were already practicing in the soccer field behind the high school.

I climbed out of the car, and Mr. Harper pulled a

black-and-blue jersey over my T-shirt. "You're captain of the Eagles," he said, tugging the shirt down over me. "And you're playing the Jaguars. Here comes Coach Winicky."

"Yo, Hardy!" The coach, a young man with long blond hair flying behind his head, wearing a black-and-blue sweatsuit, came trotting toward us. He bumped fists with me. "I was worried about you. You know we're all counting on you to have a big game."

"Uh . . . well . . ." I didn't know what to say. I knew Hardy must be a great player. But at my school, they kick *me* around instead of the ball.

Would having a new body make a big difference?

"You're our star," Winicky said. "I know you're going to pull us through and give us a big win." He bumped fists again, spun around, and ran back to the other team members.

"Go get 'em," Mr. Harper said.

I started to trot over the grass. My legs and feet felt so heavy, I kept losing my balance. The other Eagles all greeted me with shouts and fist bumps. Of course, I didn't know their names. So I had to totally fake it.

The game started. In the first few minutes, I missed a pass. I tried to send the ball to a teammate but tripped over it. I let another pass roll past me. Then I tried to kick an easy goal from in front of the net. Missed the ball and fell on my butt.

After I let a Jaguar player sail right past me and score a goal, I heard a loud whistle. It was Coach Winicky calling a time-out.

He motioned me to the sideline and put an arm around my shoulder. "Do you feel okay, Hardy?" he asked. "You've never played like this. Are you sick?"

I wanted to say, *I know I look like Hardy, but I have another brain inside me, and it's not used to playing soccer.* But *no way* I could say that.

"Just having a bad day," I muttered.

"You can turn it around," Winicky said. "I know you can." He gave me a push back onto the field.

He was wrong. I couldn't turn it around. I was terrible.

Yes, I had the right body for a star athlete. But I didn't have the brain to make the body work.

We lost the game, and my Eagle teammates circled me, shaking their heads and scowling and muttering rude words. For a moment, I thought they were going to jump on me and pound me as black and blue as the team jerseys. But they just wanted to let me know how much I had let them down.

I slumped back to Hardy's parents. They were waiting at the car, and they both kept their eyes down and avoided looking at me.

That was bad, I told myself. *But now that the game is over, I can start to enjoy being bigger and stronger.*

"We have some errands to do," Mrs. Harper said. "You can walk home. It's just two blocks that way." She told me the address and pointed down the street.

I started to walk. It was a sunny day with a cool breeze. The air felt good on my sweaty face. The game was over. I was ready to enjoy my new body. I swung my arms as my big shoes pounded the grass.

Halfway down the next block, I stopped. Three kids were standing around a tall maple tree at the curb. They were gazing up into the leaves.

A man and a woman came out of a nearby house and joined them. I moved closer and saw what they were all staring at. An orange-and-white cat gazed down at us, curled up on a high limb.

Two more kids joined the crowd. "My cat can't get down," a boy whined. His face was red. I could see he was about to burst into tears.

"We'd better call the fire department," the man said. "They'll need a tall ladder."

I realized the woman was looking at me. "Hardy," she said. She recognized me. "Hardy, you're the strongest kid here." She motioned with both hands. "Climb up and get Shawn's cat."

I took some steps back, shaking my head. "No—I—uh—I'm not a tree climber," I stammered. I was always too small to climb trees, so I never tried.

The woman squinted at me. "Hardy, I've seen you climb taller trees than this one." She motioned with both hands again. "Hurry. Get up there."

High above us, the cat let out a terrified *squawk*. Its tail poked straight up in the air, as if it was raising a flag for help.

"Pablo is scared," the little boy said, trembling. He turned to me. "Please—get him."

Did I have a choice? They thought I was Hardy and Hardy was a climber.

Okay, okay. How difficult could it be?

I took a deep breath. Then I spread my arms around the trunk, dug my sneakers into the bark, and started to work my way up. "Oww!" The bark was a lot rougher than I thought. "Cut my hand!" I cried.

A mile above me, Pablo let out another *squawk* of terror.

"Keep going, Hardy!" the woman shouted.

I had a long climb to reach the lowest limb. The jagged bark scraped my hands. I kept my eyes on the cat. I didn't look down. Did I mention I'm afraid of heights?

I had almost reached the lowest limb when I lost my grip. "Oh noooo!" I uttered a long cry as I slid all the way back to the ground. I landed on my butt with a hard *thud*.

"Stop clowning, Hardy," the woman scolded. She pulled me up by my shirt collar. "Why are you acting so weird? Get up there. Go!"

"Go! Go! Go!" The kids all started to chant.

So, okay. I took another deep breath. I wiped my sweaty hands on the legs of my jeans. And I started to inch up the tree trunk again.

"Go! Go! Go!" The kids' voices rang in my ears and drowned out the drumbeat pounding of my heart.

A little higher . . . A little higher . . .

Whoops! Almost slipped again.

I can do this, I told myself. But I didn't believe it. Even with this strong, new body.

I was inches from the bottom limb when Pablo the cat let out another loud cry. I saw something sail across the green leaves above my head. It took me a few seconds to realize it was Pablo!

The kids all screamed. I heard a soft *thud*.

I turned in time to see Pablo scampering away across the lawns.

He jumped! The cat had jumped down.

And here I was, halfway up a tree. My legs began to tremble. My breath caught in my throat. I uttered a choked cry. "Can anyone help me?" I cried in a tiny voice. "Can anyone help me down?"

The man climbed up and helped me slide down. My hands were red and sore, and my legs wouldn't stop trembling. "Hardy, you're not acting like yourself," he said.

"Tell me about it," I muttered. Being big and strong was tougher than I imagined.

I went up to Hardy's room, closed the door, and lay down on his bed to rest. I wondered how Hardy was doing in my body. I must have drifted off to sleep. I was awakened sometime later by a tangy aroma floating in through the open bedroom window.

I peered out the window down to the backyard. Hardy's dad stood at a large barbecue grill, waving a metal spatula as hamburgers sizzled in front of him.

My stomach growled. I realized I was hungry. My mouth started to water at the thought of a big, juicy cheeseburger with ketchup.

I hurried outside. The Harpers had a picnic table on their patio. Mrs. Harper sat at the table watching Hardy's dad as he flipped the burgers.

"Just in time," he said to me. "I knew the smell would bring you down here."

He picked up a plate with three buns on it. Then he scooped three cheeseburgers off the grill and placed them on the buns. "Here you go," he said. "Here's a start."

I stared at the three huge burgers. "A start?"

Mr. Harper nodded. "It's okay. You know you can come back for more."

I made a gulping sound. "But—"

"Go sit down," he said. "Hardy always has three cheeseburgers and a big dessert."

"But—but—" I sputtered. "Do I have really have to—?"

He gave me a gentle shove toward the picnic table. "Every bite. You've got to keep Hardy's strength up."

He ate two cheeseburgers. Mrs. Harper ate one. And they wouldn't let me get up from the table until I somehow stuffed all three burgers down my throat.

Whoa. Can you guess who was sick all night?

I tried to throw up quietly so they wouldn't know. I felt so heavy, like I had swallowed a bowling ball. I could barely make it back and forth to the bathroom.

I was up all night, holding Hardy's stomach with both hands. I couldn't wait to get back to my body. I no longer cared about being big or little or anything in between. I just wanted to be myself again.

The next morning at Mind Blowers my parents were already waiting. Poochy barked and cried and jumped all over me. Mom and Dad hugged me as if I'd been gone for a year.

I gazed across the room at my body with Hardy inside it. I couldn't wait to get back inside.

Hardy was complaining to his parents. "All day, I felt so cramped in here," he whined, tapping his chest. "What a tight squeeze. I can't wait to be me again."

Dr. Ripple appeared in her white lab coat. She glanced at her watch. "Time to switch back, boys," she said. "I hope you had a fun day yesterday."

I started to walk into one end of the curtained booth. But Hardy raised a hand. "I just have to run to the bathroom," he said. "I'll be right back. Don't start without me."

Don't start without me?

I think that was his idea of a joke. He turned and ran to the door at the far end of the room.

I stepped into the booth. My heart was pounding in my chest, and my hands were cold and damp. I guess I was nervous. I couldn't wait to be Skippy again.

I sat down on the wooden stool and pulled the headphones over my head. I clasped and unclasped my hands in my lap. I tapped my foot . . . nervous . . . waiting.

Finally, I heard sounds from the other side of the booth. I knew that Hardy inside my body must be ready. Finally.

I took a deep breath. Shut my eyes. And pressed the red button.

Once again, I felt a jolt, a powerful burst of wind against my back that almost sent me tumbling off the stool. A shrill screech in my ears made me cry out. White lights swirled around me.

Gasping for breath, I waited for it all to stop. Then I dropped onto the floor and crawled out of the booth.

To my surprise, Dr. Ripple and the four parents all gaped at me in horror. "I'm so sorry. I—I couldn't keep Poochy out of the booth!" my dad stammered. "He went in the other side."

"You didn't push the button, did you?" Dr. Ripple said. "Please tell me you didn't push the button."

"Rrrrrffff!" I answered. "Rrrrrrarrrrf. Roooorrffffff rfffff!"

THE STOPWATCH

I love stories about time. I can't read enough stories about time travel. I'd love to travel back in time for just a few hours to see what it was like.

And I love stories about time stopping. Or time speeding up. Or people losing track of time.

In the first Stinetinglers book, I wrote a story called "Welcome to the In-Between." It's about a boy who is trapped in time—the clock doesn't move for him. Everyone else goes about their life. But he keeps repeating the same hour.

For this book, I asked myself, "What if I reverse it? Everyone *else* gets frozen in time except for the star of the story?"

Can you guess what happens to him?

I WAS SUPPOSED TO MOW THE BACKYARD, AND I DIDN'T. IT GAVE Dad an excuse to tell me all that's wrong with me.

"I don't like to lecture you . . ." That's how he started. But he really does like to lecture me. And once he gets started listing all the bad things I've done, it's hard for him to stop.

Don't get me wrong. He's a good guy and a good dad. He's a high school teacher, and he lectures all day long. And I guess it's hard for him to stop lecturing when he's home.

I'm Eli Fortunato. *Fortunato* means "lucky" in Italian. I'm not exactly the luckiest twelve-year-old in the world. That's because of Mac and Zack, the Vossel twins.

They were the reason I didn't have a chance to mow the lawn.

I was on my way home from a friend's house when the

Vossel twins cornered me and forced me to play soccer with them. Mainly, they used me as a soccer ball.

Mac and Zack like to play rough. Especially with me. Ask me how I spell the word *bullies*. I spell it *V-o-s-s-e-l*.

Our teacher, Ms. Silber, spent a whole morning talking about bullying and how bad it is. But guess what? The Vossel twins were absent that day.

To be totally honest, I live in terror because of them.

I tried to tell my dad about them. I told him how they like to duck my head in the water fountain at school. And how they wrote rude words on my jeans in permanent marker. How they like to trip me on the stairs to the lunchroom. And how they tied my gym clothes in knots so I missed gym class.

Know what Dad said?

"Pay them back. Give them what they gave you, Eli."

What does that *mean*? Does it make any sense at all?

There's no way I could try to pay the Vossels back and live till seventh grade.

"Dad, I'm sorry I didn't mow the lawn," I said. "But I have to get to school. I—"

"It's Saturday," Dad said. "There's no school."

"We are having a dress rehearsal of the play," I explained.

"But you're not even in it," he said. "You're just the stage manager."

"They are waiting for me to hand out the costumes," I told him.

"But I'm not finished telling you what I think of your disappointing behavior," he replied.

"Maybe you could continue your lecture at dinner," I said.

Dad would have gone on forever, but Uncle Leon suddenly appeared. "The front door was open. Hope I'm not interrupting anything," he said.

Every family should have an Uncle Leon. He's a big, friendly guy, with a white beard and twinkly blue eyes. Like Santa Claus. Always smiling and making jokes and messing with people. He likes to tease people and make them laugh. And he loves to give everyone little presents.

"Leon? What's up?" Dad said.

"I wanted to stop by and give Eli an early birthday present," he said. He patted the pocket of his baggy pants.

"But my birthday isn't for three months," I said.

His eyes flashed. "I told you it was an *early* present," he said.

Dad's phone rang. He glanced at the screen. Then he walked out of the room to answer the call.

"I think you can use this," Uncle Leon whispered. He pulled a small blue bag from his pocket. The bag had a red drawstring pulled tight on the end.

"Don't open it till later, Eli," he said, still whispering. "And whatever you do, don't use it until you've read the instructions. That's very important."

He tucked the bag into my jeans pocket.

"Thank you, Uncle Leon," I said. "I'm sorry I can't stay, but I'm late for rehearsal at school." I waved goodbye and made my way out the back door.

School is two blocks away. Since I was late, I took a shortcut and ran through backyards.

I was halfway down the second block when hands grabbed my shoulders from behind.

Mr. Preek. The mean neighbor. Does every neighborhood have one?

His hands were bony and hard. He squeezed my shoulders, then let go. He scowled at me. "Eli, how many times have I told you not to run through my backyard? You'll trample my tomato plants."

I wasn't anywhere near his tomato plants. They were way at the back of the yard. Besides, they were saggy and wilted. They looked as if they had already been trampled.

"S-sorry," I stammered. "I—I'm late." I spun away from him and took off running.

"I'm warning you," Preek shouted after me. "Next time, I'm calling the police on you for trespassing!"

This day is sure going well, I thought.

When I ran onstage in the auditorium at school, I was

sweaty and breathing hard. Ms. Silber gave me a tough time, too.

"We've all been waiting, Eli," she said. "We can't start the dress rehearsal without our costumes."

"I'm on it," I said. I trotted to the rack of costumes I had at the back of the stage. We were doing the musical *The Phantom of the Opera*, and there were a lot of costumes. Gowns and capes and fancy masks.

The Vossel twins tried to trip me as I ran past them. They were parading back and forth, practicing their lines out loud, making sure everyone saw them.

They have a way of flipping their long hair from side to side as they walk. They both love their hair. They're always fussing with it, smoothing it down, brushing it back and shaking it out.

Like they're movie stars or something.

I rolled the rack of costumes center stage and began to hand them out. Of course, there was trouble.

"I can't wear this cape," Selena Brown said. "It's too heavy. And the fabric is too scratchy. Look, Eli. I put it around my shoulders, and now I have a rash on my neck."

I groaned. "Okay. I'll see what else I have."

Selena is not my favorite person. She's a little spoiled. She's the only one who comes to school on an electric bike. And she brought a pillow from home because she said her desk chair is too hard.

I walked over to the costume rack, and I saw Mac and Zack Vossel follow me. "What's the problem?" I said.

"Our boots are too tight," Zack said. "I can't walk in these."

"Give us bigger boots," his brother said. "Hurry."

"Well . . ."

They both leaned over to pull off their boots. "Whoa!" Zack pretended to stumble. He head-bumped Mac hard. They both tumbled into the rack and knocked it over. It hit the stage floor with a deafening *crash*. Costumes spilled everywhere.

"Oops," Mac said. "An accident."

"A total accident," Zack said.

They both burst out laughing.

"You're not funny," I muttered. *No way* it was an accident.

I bent to start gathering up the costumes—and I felt a cold splash.

I turned and saw the twins had their water bottles raised. They sent cold water pouring onto the back of my pants.

Laughter rang off the stage walls. Everyone was laughing at me. I raised my eyes and saw that Selena Brown was laughing harder than anyone.

I could feel my face turn hot and I knew I was blushing. "Not funny!" I screamed. "Not funny at all!"

And that made everyone laugh even harder.

The back of my pants was soaked. I tried to ignore it and bent down to collect the costumes. I heard a soft *thump*. The blue bag had fallen from my pocket. Uncle Leon's gift.

I dropped two fur capes and picked up the bag. The drawstring had come loose, and the bag was part open. I remembered that my uncle had said not to open it. But I had to look.

I reached into the bag and pulled out the gift. It looked like a big silver coin. I turned it over in my hand and stared at the round glass cover. It took me a little while to realize it was some kind of watch.

"Strange," I murmured. The watch had only one hand. Tiny numbers went all around the watch face. "It's a stopwatch," I realized.

Weird present.

Uncle Leon said to be sure to read the instructions. I reached into the bag. Nothing else in there. Then I saw a folded-up sheet of paper on the floor.

I reached for it—and a foot stomped down on it.

Mac Vossel. "Where are my boots?" he asked.

"I need that paper," I said.

He moved his foot and lifted the instruction sheet off the floor. "You mean this?" he said. Then he ripped it in half. "Oops. It got torn."

"Give it to me!" I cried. I swiped a hand at it.

Mac ducked away and ripped it again. And again. "Whoa. Another accident," he said. He tossed the little scraps of paper off the stage. I watched them scatter over the auditorium floor.

"No! I need that!" I cried. Mac laughed.

I turned and saw Ms. Silber hurrying toward me. "Eli, we're wasting time," she said. "If you can't handle the costumes, we'll have to get someone else to be stage manager."

"No. I'm on it," I said. "No worries." I turned and picked up the two capes.

"Maybe you should go home and change your pants," the teacher said. "Did you have some kind of accident?"

More laughter.

I knew I was blushing again. I gritted my teeth to keep from screaming.

I gripped the stopwatch tightly in my fist. I moved my thumb over it and pressed the little silver stem.

AND EVERYTHING STOPPED.

Everyone froze. No one moved. The stage was instantly silent. Ms. Silber stood with her clipboard raised. The Vossel twins had their boots raised in front of them. Selena Brown froze with her mouth wide open in a laugh.

I gasped. *What happened?*

Everyone stood still as statues. It was as if I had pressed pause.

I stepped up to Ms. Silber and waved my hand in front of her face. She didn't move. Her eyes stared straight ahead. She didn't blink.

I walked up behind Zack Vossel and pushed him hard in the back. He stayed frozen. Everyone was frozen in place. Except me.

This is awesome, I thought. *It's an amazing stopwatch. It stops EVERYTHING.*

I gazed around the silent stage suddenly feeling chill after chill roll down my back. *I caused this. I stopped everything. How long will it last? What if I can't bring them back?*

I took a deep breath and held it. I gripped the stopwatch tightly. At first, I was excited. Now I was frightened.

A dozen thoughts flashed through my mind. I started to think about all the fun I could have while everyone was frozen. I could mess up the Vossel twins' perfect hair. I could put a bug in Selena Brown's open mouth . . .

How long would they stay frozen? A few minutes? *Forever?*

If only I had the instruction sheet.

I gazed at the stopwatch in my hand. *Maybe if I press the stem again, they'll start to move.*

I slid my thumb over the glass cover and pressed the stem.

Nothing happened. No one moved. All frozen. Everyone frozen.

Oh no. What have I done?

I pressed the stem twice. The stage filled with voices and noise as everyone started moving again. I breathed a long sigh.

So, that was the secret. One push to freeze everyone. Two pushes to get them moving again.

"Eli, where is the cape for Selena?" Ms. Silber asked.

"And where are our boots? We can't wear these," Mac Vossel said, waving the boots in front of him.

They didn't realize they'd been frozen.

"Hurry, Eli," Ms. Silber said. She held her clipboard in front of her and tapped it impatiently. "I shouldn't have chosen a snail to be stage manager."

"He isn't a snail," Zack Vossel said. "He's a slug."

Kids laughed.

"That's enough," I said out loud. I pressed the stem on the stopwatch.

Everyone froze again. The Vossel twins were still holding their boots. Selena Brown was caught in mid-laugh again.

Was I fed up with everyone? Three guesses. There's only so much a kid can take.

A grin spread over my face. What a perfect opportunity for some payback!

I began pacing back and forth in front of everyone. My

mind whirred with ideas about what I could do to them. One idea made me laugh out loud.

"Don't anybody move!" I shouted. That was kind of a joke.

I walked to the supply closet backstage and searched inside it until I found a hammer and some nails. My next hunt was for the Vossel twins' sneakers. I spotted them on the floor against the wall outside the dressing room.

The Vossels were always bragging about how expensive their official NBA designer sneakers were. I got down on my knees and picked them up. They were heavy. Very solid. Black and white with jagged red lightning bolts over the toes.

I set the shoes back down. Then, giggling to myself, I raised the hammer and nailed the four shoes to the floor.

I kept glancing back at the frozen twins. Would the pounding of the hammer wake them up? No. No one moved. The hammer *thuds* were the only sound in the auditorium.

Still giggling, I replaced the hammer in the closet. Then I crossed to the table in the center of the stage. A big bowl of waxed fruit stood on the table. I picked a wax apple from the bowl and stuffed it into Selena's open mouth.

Then I walked back to the rack of costumes. I took out the stopwatch and clicked it twice.

Everyone buzzed back to life. Ms. Silber tapped her

clipboard. Kids at the side of the stage adjusted their costumes. I heard a shrill scream, and I knew it was Selena.

I watched her tug the wax apple from her mouth. She made gagging sounds for a little while. "How did that get in my mouth?" she cried, spitting out chunks of wax. "Where did it come from?"

Ms. Silber shook her head. "Please don't eat the props, Selena," she said. "If you're hungry, we can get you a snack."

"But—but—but—" Selena sputtered.

I covered my mouth so no one could see me laughing.

Ms. Silber started the dress rehearsal, and it went pretty well. Most everyone remembered their lines. The teacher had to tell the Vossel twins to stop smoothing back their hair while they were in a scene. But otherwise, it was a good dress rehearsal.

Of course, I couldn't really concentrate on the play. I was waiting for it to be over so that Mac and Zack could discover their sneakers. It was all I could think about.

Ms. Silber thanked everyone for their hard work. "See you Monday for our final rehearsal," she said.

Kids removed their costumes and handed them back to me. The Vossel twins heaved their boots at me. I ducked out of the way, and they bounced across the floor.

The stage was nearly empty. Most kids had left for

home. I hung costumes on the rack and waited for the twins to find their sneakers.

I didn't have to wait long.

The screams and cries of the two brothers rang out through the auditorium.

"No way!"

"I can't believe it!"

"No way! No way!"

I stepped away from the costume rack and watched them struggling to pull their shoes from the floor. When they saw me, they stood up and came rushing at me.

"*You* did this!" Mac screamed. "You!" He raised both hands to strangle me.

I put on my innocent face. "How *could* I? You both saw me. I never went backstage. I've been here at the rack the whole time."

Their faces were an angry red. They stared at me, breathing hard. Zack let out a cry. He rushed forward and sent the costume rack slamming to the floor.

Mac swept his fist over my prop cabinet and knocked everything to the floor. Then they stomped to the back of the stage to try to free their sneakers.

I guess they haven't learned their lesson, I thought. *Oh, well. There's always tomorrow.*

I checked to make sure the stopwatch was safely tucked

into my pocket. Then I walked home, humming to myself. *The stopwatch gives me SUPERPOWERS!*

Dad greeted me at the door, and he looked angry. "Where were you, Eli? I expected you home an hour ago."

"The rehearsal went long," I said.

He frowned at me. "I don't care. If you knew you'd be late, you should have called. You have to learn—"

I squeezed the stem on the stopwatch and stopped him right there. I wanted to celebrate my victory over the Vossel twins. I didn't want to listen to another of Dad's lectures.

I left him frozen at the front door and hurried up to my room. I emailed Uncle Leon and told him how much I loved his present. Then I made my way downstairs to the kitchen. I found my dinner on the counter, took it to the table, and ate it.

Then I went back to the living room. I clicked the stopwatch twice and Dad blinked his eyes. "Where was I?" he said. "What was I talking about?"

"You were asking me how the rehearsal went," I said.

He nodded. "Oh, right. How did it go?"

The stopwatch was changing my life. No more lectures. No more bullying by the twins.

On Monday morning, I felt powerful and excited and eager to get to school.

I took my shortcut through backyards so I could get

there sooner. I was halfway across Mr. Preek's yard when he leaped out to block my path.

"Young man, I warned you," he said. "I warned you about my tomatoes. Now I'm going to call the police and—"

I clicked the stopwatch and froze him. He had a drop of spit on his chin, and it stuck right there.

I walked to his garden, and I plucked several tomatoes off their vine. Then I stuffed tomatoes in all his pockets. I pushed his pockets in so the tomato juice would seep out. Then I dropped a few tomatoes down the front of his shirt.

Giggling to myself, I ran to the next yard and hid behind a hedge. I clicked the stopwatch twice and watched Mr. Preek come to life again.

He gazed all around. I guess he wondered where I went. Then his expression changed as he realized his pockets were all wet and sticky.

I laughed all the way to school.

Our dress rehearsal was first thing. When I stepped onto the stage, the cast members were all pacing around, practicing their lines, getting ready.

The Vossel twins were parading around at the front of the stage, brushing their long hair, smoothing it down, then brushing it some more.

Selena Brown hurried up to me, holding her sparkly

rhinestone mask. "Eli, this doesn't work," she said, shoving it at me. "The rhinestones scratch my face. Do you have something smoother? Also, they're not my color. I need something paler."

Ms. Silber stepped up behind her, shaking her head. "Eli, I need to talk to you," she said. "When I arrived this morning, the props were all over the floor. Why didn't you pick them up before you left Saturday night?"

I started to tell her that Mac Vossel knocked them all on the floor. But then I decided I had something better I could do.

I pushed the little stem on my stopwatch and froze them all. The Vossel twins stood with hairbrushes in their hair. Selena had the rhinestone mask shoved toward me. Ms. Silber's face was locked in its angry scowl.

"You've all been asking for it," I told them. "I should have warned you. No more Mr. Nice Guy."

I knew they couldn't hear me. But it felt good to say it.

I could feel the excitement pulsing at my temples. My heart started to patter in my chest. My new power was simply *awesome*.

I walked to the supply closet and found a large pair of scissors. Then I walked up to the frozen Vossel twins, and I gave them both haircuts.

I snipped off all the hair on the left sides of their heads. Cut them down to the scalp. I didn't touch the right sides.

Bald on one side, long hair on the other side. Laughing out loud, I stood there for a long moment, admiring my work.

I dug in the prop cabinet for a white rubber Phantom mask. I tugged it down over Selena's head. It was very tight, much too small for her. I knew it would take her *hours* to pull it off.

Then I found the Phantom's cape and rhinestone mask, and I dressed Ms. Silber in them.

Wow. Being a stage manager was never this much fun!

Giggling to myself, I stepped into the supply closet and pulled the door almost shut. I needed a good place to watch what happened next.

I clicked the stopwatch twice, and everyone started to move.

Sabrina let out a scream. "What's happening? Help me, someone!" She tugged frantically at the mask over her face. "Help me! It's so *tight*!"

Ms. Silber stood still for a long moment. I could see she was trying to remember when she put on the mask and cape. She started to wriggle out of the cape. But she stopped and pointed at Mac and Zack.

"Oh no!" she cried. "What happened to your hair? Did you cut it?"

Mac's mouth dropped open. He stared at his brother and gasped. "Zack—your hair!"

"*Your* hair!" Zack exclaimed. "It's . . . it's gone!"

Now everyone was watching the Vossel twins. They were screaming and rubbing the bald side of their heads.

Hidden in the supply closet, I covered my mouth so no one could hear me laughing. "Awesome!" I told myself. "This is the best day of my life!"

And then I asked myself: *What else can I do?*

This was too good to quit now. Yes, everyone thought they could pick on me and make my life hard forever. But I was showing them all. *No way* I could stop now.

I squeezed the stopwatch in my hand and pressed the little stem with my thumb. "Oh no . . ." I muttered in surprise as the stem broke off the watch. I watched in shock as it fell to the closet floor and rolled out the door.

I bent to pick up the stem. But I couldn't.

I couldn't. I couldn't. I couldn't move.

From the slit in the closet door, I watched everyone. They were all talking at once, trying to figure out what had happened to them.

The Vossel twins had found a mirror backstage. They were examining their half-bald heads in horror. Selena was still struggling to pull off the rubber mask.

My hand gripped the stopwatch tightly. I tried to move my arm, but I was totally frozen. I couldn't even blink.

The broken stem, I thought. *The broken watch—it froze only me.*

Please, someone, I begged silently, *come find me. I'm frozen here in the closet. Someone please come and find the stem. Please, someone—help me!*

Then I saw Ms. Silber walking toward me, taking long strides to the closet.

Yes! She'll find me! She'll help me!

I watched the teacher stumble over something on the stage floor. She picked it up in two fingers and raised it close.

The stopwatch stem. She found the stem!

Yes! Yes! She can save me!

She squinted at it for a few seconds. Then she tossed it into the auditorium.

She turned back to the others. "Okay, get your costumes, everyone," she called. "Let's have a good rehearsal."

She glanced all around the stage. "Where is Eli? Did he disappear again? Eli? Where are you? We need you to get a move on!"

KIDS RULE

One day when I asked my grandson Dylan to stop eating candy before lunch, he scowled at me and said, "You're not the boss of me!"

That got me thinking.

Kids have been saying "You're not the boss of me" for at least a hundred years. They don't want to be bossed around. They don't want a boss.

Kids want to *be* the boss.

I started thinking: What if that happened? What if kids became the boss? What would the world be like?

And that's how this story got started.

SURE, SOME KIDS MAKE FUN OF MY NAME. IT'S SONNY. THEY
think it's a riot to call me Sonny Boy. And adults ask me,
what's my *real* name?

But I don't care. I'm actually Sonny Russell III. My grandfather was Sonny Russell and my dad is Sonny Russell Jr.

What's so funny about that?

You might say I'm a serious kid. My best friends, Enrico
and Bert, are always telling me to lighten up. But I'm a
serious inventor. I have been since I was nine. And I'd
rather work on my projects than hang out or play video
games or just about anything else.

I spend every minute I can in the workshop Mom and
Dad set up for me in the garage. I've been working for
months and months on my latest project. No joke. I think
it's going to change the world.

Enrico and Bert don't believe me. Saturday afternoon

they appeared in my garage with softball gloves and a ball and bat. I have a big backyard, and it's great for ball games. But I was trying to solve a serious problem with my invention, and I really wasn't in the mood.

Enrico grabbed my arm and started to drag me from the garage. He's bigger than me, and sometimes it makes him think he's in charge. I had a bunch of fragile microchips in my hand, and I nearly dropped them.

"Invent later," he said. "It will wait."

"I'm at an important part," I said. I tried to struggle free, but he hung on.

"Let's have fun for a change," Bert said. Bert is a good guy, but he pretty much follows whatever Enrico says. "You can hit first, Sonny."

"You don't get it," I said. "This invention is—"

"—not going to work," Enrico finished my sentence for me. Enrico talks very fast. He finishes everyone's sentences. Sometimes it sounds like he's on fast-forward. "Your inventions don't work," he said. "So you should get some fresh air instead."

"That's not true—" I started.

"How about the dog feeder?" Bert said. He rolled his eyes. "That was a real winner."

Enrico laughed. "Your dog bowl was supposed to feed a dog for a week, one meal at a time. But forget about it. Your dog ate the entire week in ten minutes."

"And now he looks like a big furry pillow," Bert said.

"Leave Cooper out of it," I muttered. "It wasn't his fault. The dog bowl had a few problems."

I wanted to tell them that this invention was different. It was going to be awesome beyond belief. But I could see their minds were set on playing ball. So I closed the garage door and followed them to the backyard.

I could see my little sister, Tessie, watching us from the kitchen window. Tessie always butts in whenever Enrico and Bert come over and messes up whatever we're trying to do. Do you know how to spell the word *pest*? I spell it *T-e-s-s-i-e*.

Luckily, she was grounded today and couldn't come outside. Tessie broke some dishes so she wouldn't have to wash them, and Mom said she was grounded at least until she's twenty-one.

I think that's too soon. But Mom and Dad told me to butt out of it.

There's a flat rock in my backyard that we use for home plate. Enrico pitched and Bert played outfield, standing where the grass ended by the fence.

Our game didn't last long. I slapped a few grounders past Enrico. Cooper got to the ball before Bert did, and we had to pry it from the dog's mouth.

Then I swung hard and hit a high fly ball that sailed over my neighbor's fence.

"Oh no," I muttered, shaking my head. Mr. Clarky, the neighbor, isn't a nice guy. I hoped maybe he wasn't home. But his bald head popped up instantly over the fence, and he wasn't smiling.

Cooper jumped at the fence and began barking his head off. He doesn't like Mr. Clarky, either.

Clarky pointed at Cooper. "Make him stop barking at me, Sonny. Or I'll call the city and have him taken away."

That's just the kind of thing a bad neighbor would say—isn't it?

Enrico and Bert pulled Cooper away from the fence.

"Sorry, Mr. Clarky," I said. "Can we have our ball back?"

"What ball?" he replied.

I could see it in his hand. "The ball you're holding," I said.

He pretended to be confused. "I don't know what you're talking about," he said. Then he held the ball up. "You mean *this* ball? I don't know who it belongs to. I just found it in my yard. Guess it's mine."

"It's our ball," I said. "Could you—"

He turned and carried the ball into his house. The door slammed behind him.

What can you do about a bad neighbor like that? I was hoping my new invention might help with the problem.

Enrico, Bert, and I were feeling sorry for ourselves. We slumped into the house. Mom was busy in the kitchen.

Tessie was helping her. "Can we have some snacks?" I asked.

She shook her head. "We're going out for dinner, Sonny. I'm sorry, but I don't want you to spoil your appetite."

"Sorry, Sonny! No snacks!" Tessie said in a sarcastic voice. She stuck her tongue out at me.

Why do adults worry so much about your appetite? And who made them the Snack Masters and gave them control over when you can have snacks?

I led the way upstairs to my room. I raised a finger to my lips to signal my two friends to be quiet. Then I opened my closet door and pulled out the hidden bag of Halloween candy I've been saving for months.

I started up the *Minecraft* game on my PlayStation and handed out a bunch of candy bars to Enrico and Bert. We sat cross-legged on the rug and began to pig out. It was turning into a pretty good afternoon.

But after twenty minutes or so, I saw a shadow move outside my bedroom window. I paused the game and crept to the window.

I can see the back of Mr. Clarky's house from my room. And there he was behind the curtains in an upstairs bedroom. He had binoculars up to his face and they were pointed right at my window.

I jumped away from the window. "Hey—Clarky is spying on us," I told my friends.

"No way," Bert said. "Why would he do that?"

"Why would he do anything?" I replied.

We started up the game again, and I passed out a few more chocolate bars. We only played another five minutes when Mom came flying into the room.

"Busted!" she cried. Her eyes were on the chocolate bars in our laps and the candy wrappers all over the floor. "Sonny, I told you no snacks. And look—"

"How did you know?" I demanded. I knew the answer.

"Mr. Clarky called from next door and said he saw you stuffing yourselves with chocolate," Mom answered. "He said he was worried you all might get sugar poisoning."

Sugar poisoning? Is that a thing?

"I can explain—" I said.

"No, you can't," Mom replied. "You deliberately disobeyed me. So, guess what? Dad and I will not take you to the Buttered Bizkitz concert next Saturday. That's your punishment."

Bert, Enrico, and I all groaned at once. "That's a terrible punishment," I cried. "You know we've been looking forward to the Buttered Bizkitz for months!"

"That's what makes it a good punishment," Mom said.

I heard Tessie's shrill laugh. I didn't even know the little punk was standing behind Mom.

Bummer. Enrico and Bert went home. And guess what? The day got worse.

A little after five, I was back in my garage workshop, having trouble with some stubborn circuits. I looked up when Dad's car pulled into the driveway.

Dad looked tired. I guess because he had to work on Saturday. He dragged his briefcase from the car, started to the house, then stopped and gazed around the backyard.

Shaking his head, he spun around and came striding over to me. "Sonny, you promised to weed the garden," he said.

I squinted at him. "Weed?"

"Are you going to pretend you forgot?" he asked.

"Forgot?"

"You promised you'd have the garden weeded by the time I got home," he said.

"Oh. Right." I snapped my fingers. "Completely forgot."

"Well, guess what, Mr. Forgetful?" he said. "I'm going to completely forget to take you to Angelo's Pizza tonight."

"But, Dad—" I pleaded. Angelo's Pizza is the *best*. But I knew there was no point pleading with Dad. Once he said something, he never changed his mind. He is a stubborn dude.

My parents are bullies, I thought bitterly. *Why do they always have to have their own way? Why are adults on such a power trip?*

It made me think about a night last week. Mom and Dad went shopping, so I had to babysit Tessie. She was in her room watching animal videos on Mom's iPad. So I figured she'd be okay if I went out to the garage and did some electrical work on my new project.

Big mistake. When I came back in the house, Tessie had taken red and yellow markers and drew flowers all over the living room wall.

What was she *thinking*?

Was she just trying to get me in trouble? Well, if so, it worked.

I got blamed. I didn't do it, but Mom and Dad said I was in charge. So it was my fault, and I had to be punished.

Of course, that was totally unfair. But it's just the way parents work. Sometimes parents are out of control.

And that also goes for Mr. Schlitz, my sixth-grade teacher.

Okay. Maybe the whole thing was partly my fault.

A few weeks ago, I built a little sound effects box in my workshop, and I wanted to try it out. I sneaked it into Schlitz's classroom and hid it under his desk.

It had a Bluetooth controller that I hid in my pocket. When Mr. Schlitz started class, he sat down on the edge of his desk. "Good morning, everyone," he said.

I pushed a button and the box under his desk blasted the sound of a squealing pig.

It was a riot. It sounded like a pig with its foot caught in a car door.

Mr. Schlitz blinked in surprise and jumped to his feet. "As I started to say—"

I pushed the button again, and the loud pig squeal made him gaze all around in confusion.

A lot of kids were laughing. He turned and searched his desktop. Of course, he couldn't find anything.

I blasted another pig squeal.

Now everyone was laughing. Schlitz's face darkened to deep red. He lowered himself behind his desk—and found the box.

Of course, he knew who had put it there. He called me out of class and yelled at me for a long while. My parents had to come to school to discuss it with him.

Believe that? It was just a joke, after all.

"You're a smart kid, Sonny," Schlitz said. "But you have to learn to take life more seriously."

Why?

It was one more example of adults wanting to control everything.

That's why I've been so eager to finish my invention. You can't imagine how *psyched* I was a few days later when it was finally ready to show to my friends. I could barely breathe when Bert and Enrico arrived at my garage.

They both stopped several feet away from it and stared hard. I had the invention standing in the middle of the garage. It was about six feet tall and four feet wide.

"It's . . . a mirror?" Bert asked finally.

"It's a digital mirror," I said. "You can see your reflection in it. But you can also step into it."

They studied their reflections for a while. Enrico scratched his head. "What is it? What does it do?" he demanded.

"I call it a World Reverser," I said. "Mirrors reverse everything, right? They reverse the whole world."

They both looked totally confused. "So?" Bert said. "So what?"

"I'll demonstrate," I said. I was so eager to show it off, my legs were shaking. "Come on. Step into the mirror. You'll see what it does."

They both hung back. "Is it safe?" Enrico asked.

"It's electric, right?" Bert said. "We'll get a shock."

Before I could answer them, Tessie came racing into the garage. "I'll try it!" she cried. She lowered her shoulders and roared forward.

I grabbed her just before she ran through the mirror. "No way!" I shouted. "No way you're doing this with us."

I gripped her shoulders and spun her toward the house. "Get going, Tessie," I said. "I built this to reverse *you*!" I gave her a gentle shove to the garage door.

She shook her fists, but then took off running to the house.

I turned to my friends. "Are you coming? Let's go before that pest comes back."

They didn't move.

"I . . . don't . . . think so," Bert said, backing up a step. "It's too weird, Sonny. Walk into a mirror?"

I let out a long whoosh of air. "Okay, okay," I said. "I'll go first. I'll show you it's perfectly safe."

I couldn't wait any longer. I strode up to the mirror, raised my left leg, leaned forward—and walked into it. A low buzzing sound rang in my ears, and my whole body tingled.

My vision blurred for a second. I blinked a few times to clear my eyes. Then I turned around and faced my two friends. We stared at one another, me on one side of the mirror and them on the other.

"Can you hear us?" Bert asked.

I nodded. "Of course."

I crossed my arms in front of me. "Are you coming or not?" I said. I was starting to get impatient.

"I guess so," Bert said. He and Enrico stepped forward together. They hesitated for a few seconds. Then they both shut their eyes and walked into the mirror.

I stretched out my arms. "Here we are," I said. "In Reverse World. Awesome, right?"

They were blinking and rubbing the tingling feeling from their arms.

Bert glanced around. "Is everything really reversed?"

"Let's test it," I said. "Let's play ball."

They'd left the bat and ball and gloves in the garage. We picked them up and made our way to the backyard.

Enrico laughed. "Everything is the same, Sonny. Looks like your invention is another flop."

"Too bad," Bert said. "You worked on this for so long. And we walked through it and nothing happened." He shook his head. "Maybe you need a new hobby."

I stepped up to the flat rock, our home plate. "Not so fast," I said. "Check it out. I'm batting left-handed. That's a change, right?"

Enrico pulled his arm back to pitch the ball to me. "Oh, wow, I'm pitching left-handed," he said. "I don't believe it."

"We're reversed," Bert said. "Definitely reversed."

I swung the bat a few times. "Just pitch the ball," I told Enrico.

He reared back and sent it flying toward me. I swung hard and connected with a loud *whack*.

"Oh nooo!" I watched the ball sail over Mr. Clarky's fence. Then I heard a crash and the sound of shattering glass. "Oh wow! I don't believe it! I broke his window!"

I heard an angry shout from inside the house. The three of us froze. Clarky came running out, his face red as a tomato. He gripped the ball in one fist.

"Mr. Clarky—" I started.

He waved the ball in my face. "I'm so sorry," he said. "Did my window get in the way of your game?"

Was that a joke?

Clarky handed me the ball. "Truly sorry, Sonny," he said. "Wait here, guys. I'll be right back."

Enrico, Bert, and I stood watching him as he trotted back to his house. A few seconds later, he came hurrying back, his arms loaded down with something.

Candy bars.

"Here you go," Clarky said, handing them out. "Take these. This is for spoiling your game."

He dropped three chocolate bars into my hands. I knew I should thank him, but I was too stunned to speak.

At that moment, the back door swung open, and Cooper came running out. The big dog spotted Mr. Clarky and, barking ferociously, came running for him.

Clarky's eyes went wide, and he took a step back.

Cooper yowled and growled at him, as if ready to attack.

Clarky raised both hands in front of him. "I'm so sorry," he said. "I didn't mean to upset your dog. Please don't call the police on me. I promise I'll try to be a better neighbor."

I grabbed Cooper's collar and pulled him back. Clarky turned and hurried back to his house. Enrico and Bert were staring at their candy bars.

"Sonny, your mirror—" Bert started.

"Maybe you really did reverse everything," Enrico said, shaking his head.

They followed me as I led Cooper back into the house. My dad was watching a hockey game on TV in the den. He jumped up when the three of us appeared.

"Hey, I'm sorry, Sonny," he said. "I know I should be out weeding the garden. But I got caught up in the game. Please don't be angry."

My two friends and I exchanged glances. This was too good to be true.

"That's okay, Dad," I said. "But don't let it happen again."

He raised his right hand. "I won't. I swear. I'll have the job done in time to drive you all to the Buttered Bizkitz concert at the stadium."

Yay. The concert is *on*!

"Well, don't rush it, Dad," I said. "Do a good job. I don't want to see any weeds or crabgrass poking up."

He lowered a hand to my shoulder. "I'll do my best, Sonny. I really will," he said. "Just promise you won't get angry."

What could be better?

After he left the room, we cheered and did a happy dance and slapped high-fives and cheered some more.

Mom called us into the kitchen for lunch. She had made her famous homemade salami pizza. We ate the entire pizza and then dumped our candy bars on the table and quickly devoured them for dessert.

Mom stood at the end of the table and frowned at us. "Are you boys out of candy bars?" she asked. "I'll run to the store and get more." She started out of the kitchen but stopped at the doorway and turned back to us. "Please don't be angry. I'll only be a few minutes."

A few seconds later, we heard her car start up. We cheered and danced and slapped high-fives again. "This is awesome!" Bert exclaimed. "You did it, Sonny. Kids rule! You're a total genius!"

I had to agree with him. In school, my reverse mirror kept doing its job.

We were doing science, but I was daydreaming about what my next invention should be. It took me a while to realize that Mr. Schlitz was calling on me.

"Sonny, tell us the main points of the chapter we read last night."

I swallowed. "Uh . . . well . . . I got hung up and I didn't read the chapter," I said.

"Oh, wow," Mr. Schlitz replied. He slapped his forehead. "I must be giving too much homework. I'm so sorry, Sonny." He thought for a moment. "Tell you what, everyone," he said finally. "No more homework for the rest of the year."

The class cheered.

"I've been working you too hard," Schlitz added. "Why don't you all go home early? Enjoy the sunshine!"

Enrico and Bert kept slapping me on the back, telling me how great I was as we walked to my house. "You're a genius! A genius!" they kept exclaiming.

I don't think I ever felt happier.

That feeling ended quickly when we reached my house and saw the black-and-white police car in the driveway. "Huh?" I gasped. "What's going on?"

I burst through the front door. My two friends followed close behind.

Mom and Dad turned as I came in. Their faces were twisted in sadness and shock. Tessie was crying on the stairs.

My parents' hands were handcuffed behind their backs. And two dark-uniformed police officers were pushing them toward the door.

I could feel my heart skip a beat. "Mom! Dad!" I cried. "What is happening? Officer, what did they *do*?"

One of the officers turned to me. "They weren't nice enough to you kids," he said. "So we're taking them in. A few years in prison will teach them to obey their kids."

"We'll do better. I promise," Dad said.

"Too late for that," the other cop said. They pushed Mom and Dad out the door.

Tessie buried her face in her hands. She was sobbing loudly. "What can we do? What can we do?" she wailed.

I turned to Enrico and Bert. "I know what we can do," I said. "Follow me."

I led them into the garage. "We have to go back through the mirror," I said. "Back to the real world."

"But it's so totally awesome here," Enrico said. "Maybe we could stay a little longer and—"

"You're kidding, right?" I said. "I can't let my parents go to prison. We have to go through the mirror and reverse everything back the way it was."

They knew we had no choice. We stepped up to the mirror. Our faces stared back at us as we moved up close. "See you on the other side," I said.

I took a big step forward—and my face bumped hard against the mirror. I tried again. I took a big step and banged into the mirror.

No. No. No. I couldn't get through. The mirror felt solid.

"What's wrong?" Enrico asked.

I pushed at the mirror with both hands. I lowered my shoulder and shoved against it with all my might.

"Can't get through," I told them. "It . . . it's solid." Sweat poured down my forehead. My shoulder ached.

They both dove forward and shoved themselves against the mirror. They bumped hard and staggered back.

They stared at me. No one was smiling. "Sonny, you built a one-way mirror," Bert said.

Enrico lowered his head. "What are we going to do?" he muttered.

My mind was spinning. "It—wasn't supposed to work this way," I stammered.

"How can we get back?" Bert's voice cracked. "We have to get back."

"What about the power cable?" Enrico asked. "It's electric, right? Can't we just shut off the power?"

I sighed. "The power cable is on the other side. We can't reach it from here."

We stared at our reflections for a long time. "I don't believe this," Bert muttered. "I can't believe we're trapped here."

"Trapped here for how long?" Enrico asked. "Forever?"

I heard a sound and turned toward the house. The kitchen door swung open, and Tessie came walking out.

"Tessie! Hey—Tessie!" I shouted.

She walked into the garage and squinted at us in the mirror. "Hey—cool!" she cried.

"Tessie, wait—" I said.

She shuffled up to the mirror. "I'm coming in with you."

"No! Wait! Stop!" I shouted.

"You can't stop me. I want to come with you."

"No!" I waved both hands above my head. "Please! Stay

there! Don't come in. Listen to me, Tessie. We need you to turn it off."

She pressed her face closer. "Turn it off?"

I nodded. "Yes. See that big white cable on the side of the mirror?"

She turned. "Yes. I see it."

"You just have to unhook it," I said. "Grab it and unhook it."

"Why?" she replied.

"Don't ask questions. Please, Tessie. We're trapped here. You'll save us all. We'll be so happy. I'll do whatever you want for a year! Promise."

"So will I!" Enrico exclaimed.

"Me too," Bert said.

She stared at the cable. Then she turned and peered into the mirror at the three of us.

"Please unhook it," I begged. "Unhook it and turn off the mirror."

"Please—" Enrico echoed.

She stared at us some more. Then she reached for the cable. Her hand wrapped around it.

I held my breath. I didn't blink. I didn't move.

"Please . . . please . . ."

She pulled her hand away from the cable. "I don't want to," Tessie said. And she leaped through the mirror. She came barreling into me, and we both toppled onto the garage floor.

With an angry cry, I shoved her off me and scrambled to my feet. "Do you realize what you've done?" I screamed, shaking my fists at her. "We're trapped now and—"

I stopped because I heard footsteps. I turned to see Mr. Clarky come running toward us. "I heard your voices," he said. "Why are you kids out here in the garage so late? Is there a problem?"

"Well . . . uh . . . ." I didn't know what to say. The others just stared at him open-mouthed.

"What can I do to help you?" Clarky asked. "Can I build a tent so you can sleep in the backyard? I have a pie in the oven. I'll run to the store and buy ice cream so you can have it with the pie."

He gazed at us, moving from one to the other. "Is there anything else I can get you while I'm at the store? Do you need more candy bars?"

He couldn't help us. He was inside the mirror. He couldn't reach the plug. We watched him in silence as he drove away.

I turned and stepped up to my workbench. I reached into the drawer and began to pull out supplies.

"Sonny, what are you doing?" Enrico asked. "Are you going to work on something now?"

I nodded. "Yes," I said. "There's only one way to get back to the real world. I have to build another mirror."

Bert squinted at me. "How long will it take?"

I thought for a minute. "The first one took two years," I said. "But I remember a lot of it. Maybe I can build a new one in *one* year."

"A whole year?" Tessie cried.

"YAAAAY!" Enrico and Bert both let out a cheer and jumped up and down. "A whole year! Kids rule! Kids rule!"

SPIDER SALAD

Do you have a problem with spiders?

A lot of people do. When people make a list of the things they're afraid of, spiders are nearly always at the top of the list.

There are lots of creepy spider stories. Some of them may be true. I've read stories about spiders that crawl into someone's ear at night and lay hundreds of spider eggs. Later, the tiny spiders come pouring out.

I decided I'd write my own spider story for this book. It isn't true.

But I think you'll find it creepy. Cover your ears when you read it!

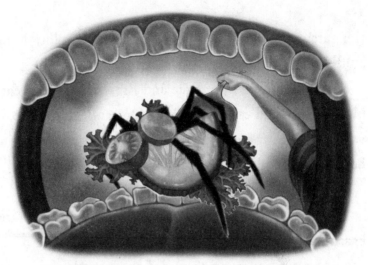

A LOT OF PEOPLE ARE AFRAID OF SPIDERS.

Maybe because they bite. Or maybe because they're ugly, and they look so menacing, sliding down from the sticky webs they make.

Or maybe spiders just have a bad reputation. Like snakes or bats or other innocent creatures that end up in scary movies and make people scream.

I'm Van Siderman. I've thought a lot about spiders. I even wrote a long report about them for Ms. Macy, my sixth-grade teacher.

But that's another story.

I guess my story begins in the playroom in my garage. That's where I was when my so-called friends Ari Becker and Lindy-Sue Moon came over to my house.

I shouldn't call it a playroom. It's actually a little apartment that my mom and dad built for me on one side of the garage. It's my own space. I hang there a lot, doing stuff.

It's a real escape from Bree and Breana, my four-year-old twin sisters. I call them Thing One and Thing Two. If you lived with them, you'd know why. And it's a place to be by myself and do whatever I want.

I call it my Me-Cave.

Mom and Dad dragged out two old armchairs from the basement for my Me-Cave. And they built a long desk out of lumber we had lying around. I bring my laptop there. I can use the Wi-Fi from the house. I even have a little mini-fridge where I keep juice and water.

My apartment has no windows. Total privacy. Which I really like.

Mom says I spend too much time by myself in there. She says I should be hanging out with Ari and Lindy-Sue and my other friends and just be outdoors and in the fresh air.

"But you worked so hard to build it for me," I say. "Don't you want me to enjoy it?"

Dad thinks it's great that I like being with myself so much. He says a lot of kids aren't self-reliant. I guess that means they need to have others around all the time.

Well, the afternoon that Ari and Lindy-Sue came by, I was in my apartment adding things to my collection. What collection? It's a secret. I told you, I like my privacy.

Mom called me into the house. She knew I wouldn't let my friends into my private space.

"Want to go to a movie?" Lindy-Sue asked. "My mom is driving us to the Metroplex."

Lindy-Sue is the tallest person in our class. She's even taller than Ms. Macy, and I don't think she likes it. She always keeps her head down low, like she's ducking from something. Trying to be shorter, I guess, even though everyone tells her it's nice to be tall.

"My cousin Gabe works behind the popcorn counter," Ari said. "If he's in a good mood, maybe he'll give us free popcorn."

"What movie?" I asked.

"The new Spider-Man," Lindy-Sue answered.

I swallowed. "I don't think so."

"I know you have a problem with spiders," Lindy-Sue said. "But it's about Spider-Man, not spiders."

"I know the origin story," I said. "Remember? A radioactive spider bit Peter Parker." I shook my head. "No thanks."

"But don't you want free popcorn?" Ari asked. He likes free stuff. He talks about getting free stuff a lot.

Mom tilted her head the way she always does when she's disappointed. "Why don't you go, Van? Everyone loves those movies."

"I'm kinda busy," I said.

"Tell you what," Mom said, turning to my two friends. "Why don't you come for lunch on Saturday? I make homemade pizza every Saturday. That way, you three could spend time together."

"Sounds like a plan," I said before Lindy-Sue or Ari could answer. And I hurried back to my Me-Cave in the garage.

Saturday afternoon, I was in my little apartment when I heard a knock on the door. I turned off the lights and slipped out the door to greet Lindy-Sue and Ari.

"Can we see your place?" Lindy-Sue asked.

They're always asking to see it. I don't know why. They know the answer.

I clicked the door shut behind me. "I'm ready for pizza," I said. "I think Mom's in the kitchen."

"But we want to see your place," Lindy-Sue insisted. "Come on, Van."

"What don't you understand about the word *private*?" I said.

Without warning, they both bumped me out of the way and charged the door. Ari grabbed the doorknob and tried to turn it. He tried a few times.

"It's locked," I said. "The door locks automatically."

Lindy-Sue stared down at me. "But—why?"

I shrugged. "That's just the way I am," I said.

Ari let go of the doorknob. "What do you *do* in there?" he demanded.

"Private things," I replied.

I led the way to the kitchen. Mom was just taking the pizza out of the oven. She slid it onto a carving board. "Have to let it cool a bit."

"Oh, it smells so good," Lindy-Sue said, sitting down next to me at the kitchen table. Ari took the chair at the end.

"I use two different cheeses and very spicy salami," Mom said. "That's what makes my pizza so different."

She carried our large wooden salad bowl to the table and set it down in front of Ari. "We always have salad first," she said. "Hope you like French dressing." She handed Ari two long salad spoons. "Ari, would you mix the salad while I slice the pizza?"

Why did Ari have that strange smile on his face? A smile I'd never seen before. I noticed it as he started to stir the salad. Then I forgot about it.

"Van won't let us see his apartment," Lindy-Sue told my mom. "We practically begged him."

"My son is weird," Mom said. She rolled the pizza slicer back and forth, cutting the pizza into triangles. Then she sat down and passed small salad bowls to Ari.

He filled the bowls and handed one to each of us. And I saw that grin again. And he and Lindy-Sue exchanged glances. But I didn't think anything of it.

I'm not a salad person. I think lettuce is for rabbits. So I always try to gulp it down as fast as I can. I like the cherry tomatoes. They're juicy and sweet. But that's about all.

I stirred the salad around, mixing the dressing over the lettuce.

I dug the fork into the salad. Started to raise a chunk to my mouth.

Stopped—and let out a cry.

My fork went flying. I knocked the salad bowl over. Lost my balance and nearly toppled off my chair.

I jumped to my feet. "Spider!" I shouted. I pointed into the pile of lettuce I'd spilled on the table. "Look at it! A spider in my salad!"

The fat black spider was balancing itself on a slice of carrot. The spindly legs were covered in French dressing.

Mom gasped. "That's impossible—!"

Ari and Lindy-Sue both burst out laughing. They bumped fists over the table.

Now I knew why they had been grinning. They added the spider to my salad.

"It's not funny!" I shouted. "I . . . I could have *eaten* it!"

That made them laugh again. And was that a smile on Mom's face?

"Bye," I said. I knew I was making too big a deal, but I couldn't help it. I grabbed a slice of pizza off the cutting board and hurried to my Me-Cave.

Monday morning in school, I was still thinking about the spider in my salad.

I thought maybe Lindy-Sue and Ari would call or text me to apologize. But they didn't. I guess they were pleased with themselves. Their spider trick got just the reaction they were looking for.

I scolded myself for falling into their trap. I should have just ignored the spider. Or maybe made a joke about it. I remember a good joke I read once . . .

A man eating in a restaurant says, "Waiter, what is this fly doing in my soup?"

And the waiter says, "It's doing the backstroke, sir."

Yes. I should have joked. But I was too startled, I guess. And I do have a thing about spiders.

I pulled some books from my locker and shoved them into my backpack. I turned to go to class when a kid I knew came walking by. DeJuan Gaines. He gave me a wave as he passed by, and said, "Hey, Spiderman!"

"Huh?" I blinked a few times. "My name is Siderman— not Spiderman."

He laughed and kept walking. Of course he knew my right name. DeJuan and I have been in the same class since second grade.

A few minutes later, when I stepped into Ms. Macy's room, a couple of kids shouted, "Yo, Spiderman! Hey— Spiderman." And I realized that Lindy-Sue and Ari had spread the word. They must have told everyone about the spider in my salad and how I spilled the salad and nearly fell off my chair.

Well, I wasn't happy, but I can take a joke. Sure, my name sounds like Spiderman. Actually, it's not a bad nickname. Van Spiderman. It's kind of cool.

I put the whole spider thing out of my mind till gym class.

In the locker room, I stepped up to my locker to get my gym clothes. I pulled open the locker door—and let out a startled scream.

A huge black spider sat on top of my gym shorts.

It took me only a few seconds to see that it was fake. A big rubber spider.

But I had already screamed. And I heard guys laughing all down the row of lockers.

Someone slapped me on the back. I spun around. Ari. His grin was so wide, it looked like his face might crack in half. "Spiderman strikes again!" he said.

I decided to put an end to the spider stuff. I grabbed

Ari by the shoulders and shoved him up against the lockers. Shoved him hard and held him there.

His eyes went wide. "Hey, Van—it was just a joke," he said. He squirmed a bit, but I didn't let go.

I pushed my face close to his and put on a good tough-guy expression. "Why?" I said, talking through gritted teeth. "Why are you and Lindy-Sue doing this to me?"

"Well . . ." I could see he was surprised by my anger.

"You two were always my friends," I said. "Why did you decide to be bullies to me now?"

"We're *not* being bullies!" he shouted. He pushed my hands away and rubbed his shoulders. "Seriously. We're not bullies," he said in a lower voice. "We're trying to help you."

"Huh? *Help* me?" I cried. "How?"

"Help you get over your fear of spiders," he said.

The bell rang. We were the only ones in the locker room.

"What makes you think I'm afraid of spiders?" I demanded.

He shook his head. "Van, don't be afraid to admit it. Lindy-Sue and I want to help you."

I gazed at the huge rubber spider sitting in my gym locker. "Are you kidding me?" I said. "I'm supposed to believe that? You're both just having fun trying to scare me."

He opened his mouth to reply. But Coach Melendez poked his head into the locker room and shouted at us. "Hey, you two! Did you forget we have a volleyball game this morning? How would you both like to do five laps around the gym to warm up?"

"Coming," Ari and I said in unison.

The coach disappeared back to the gym. I picked up the rubber spider and heaved it across the room.

At home, the twins came running from the kitchen to greet me. "Spiderman! Spiderman!" they both shouted. They surrounded me, one in front, one in back, dancing around me, laughing and chanting, "Spiderman! Spiderman!" Like it was a hilarious joke.

Where did they hear it?

Mom appeared in the kitchen doorway. "Make them stop!" I shouted. I covered my ears. "Come on. Make them stop!"

"Spiderman! Spiderman!" They began punching me with their little fists in rhythm with their chant.

"Van, you have to learn to take a joke," Mom said.

"No, I don't!" I screamed. I tossed my backpack to the floor and ran out the back door to my apartment in the garage.

I slammed the door behind me and dropped into an armchair. I covered my ears. I could still hear the girls chanting from the house.

I tried to concentrate on my collection. But I couldn't keep their laughter and shrill voices from my mind.

In school the next day, Ms. Macy was assigning science projects. She called me to her desk, then walked me over by the supply closet to talk privately.

"Am I in trouble?" I asked.

She laughed. "No. Why do you say that?"

I shrugged. "I don't know."

She narrowed her eyes at me, like she was studying me. "Van, I understand you have a problem with spiders," she said in a low voice.

"Who told you that?" I snapped. "Lindy-Sue? Ari?"

"It doesn't matter," she said. "I've given it a lot of thought. And I think your science project should be about spiders."

I blinked. "Excuse me?"

"I want you to work with Lindy-Sue and Ari on a study about spiders. I think it will help you. You'll be glad."

She waited for me to reply. But I didn't know what to say.

The spider thing was out of control. Everyone I knew was teasing me about spiders and calling me Spiderman instead of Siderman. And it was all Lindy-Sue and Ari's fault.

And now she wanted me to work on a science project with them about spiders. My mind was spinning.

Oh, well . . . I decided finally. *Maybe after we do our project together, it will put an end to the spider thing once and for all.*

"Sounds good," I told Ms. Macy.

The three of us met after school at Lindy-Sue's house. They wanted to meet at my Me-Cave. But, of course, that's still off-limits.

We sat cross-legged on the floor in the den with a big bowl of popcorn between us. I checked it first. Pawed through it carefully, looking for spiders. I could never be too sure what these two might do.

"I really need an A on this," Lindy-Sue said. "I got behind on my science notebook, and Ms. Macy said it was the worst one in the class."

"How should we get started?" I said. "I think we don't want to do a slide presentation. That's boring. We need live spiders to go with our report."

Ari slapped my shoulder. "Yeah. Definitely. Live spiders. Good attitude, Van."

Lindy-Sue swallowed a mouthful of popcorn. "Ari and I can make it easy for you," she said.

I squinted at her. "What do you mean?"

"We can collect the spiders," she replied. "You don't have to. We'll gather the spiders, and you can write the report."

"You're the best report writer," Ari said. "And you like to do research. So you write the report, and we'll gather a whole bunch of spiders."

I stared at him. Were they trying to pull something? Was this some kind of trap?

I decided they were trying to be nice. "Sounds good," I said finally.

"I have a terrific glass case to keep them in," Ari said. "It used to be my dad's terrarium. But everything in it died."

"You have the hard part," I told them. "Writing a report is easy."

"Glad you like the plan," Lindy-Sue said. "Maybe this project will help you. You know. About spiders."

"Maybe," I said.

I already know a lot about spiders. I even have a large book, an encyclopedia of spiders that I keep in my

Me-Cave. I look through it whenever I want a good shiver.

But I went online and did a lot of research. I actually filled ten pages—single-spaced—with info about spiders. I spent a week reading up about them. Then I decided I was ready to write the report.

I sat down at my laptop with my research papers next to me and started to write . . .

You'll probably be surprised by this. But there are 43,000 different kinds of spiders in the world.

If you are like me, when you think of spiders, you probably think about spider bites. A lot of people are scared of spiders. Many people think spider bites can be deadly.

But the truth is, there are only nine spider species that can kill humans.

One of the deadliest is the wolf spider. It can be found everywhere in the world. It's called the wolf spider because, like a wolf, it can run through grass very fast. And it has a habit of chasing after and pouncing on its prey.

I knew kids would like to hear about the deadly spiders in the world. So I wrote mainly about the poisonous ones than can kill humans. I left out all the boring spider info that everyone usually puts in reports.

I wrote till midnight two nights in a row. When I finished, I read the report over carefully. I had to admit it was pretty good.

I couldn't wait for us to present our project to the class. For two reasons. One, I thought everyone would be impressed with my research. And two, I hoped it would finally put an end to Ari and Lindy-Sue bullying me about spiders.

When Ms. Macy called the three of us to the front of the room to present our project, I wasn't as nervous as I thought I might be. My mouth was a little dry, but I didn't feel shaky or weird.

Ari carried a glass case between his hands. He didn't bring it too close to me. I guess because of my thing about spiders. But I could see at least twenty or thirty black and brown spiders climbing on the glass.

Good work, Ari and Lindy-Sue!

The three of us stood side by side in front of the tall bookcase beside Ms. Macy's desk. Ari set the glass spider case on top of the bookcase.

"Those are terrific spiders you brought in," Ms. Macy said. "I know everyone can't wait to hear what you have to say about them."

I raised the report in front of me and cleared my throat, ready to begin reading. The class was very quiet. I gazed around and saw that everyone was staring intently at the spiders.

I cleared my throat again and began to read. "You'll probably be surprised by this. But there are forty-three thousand different kinds of spiders in the world."

A few kids murmured their surprise at the big number.

I started the part about the wolf spiders. I knew everyone would like this part.

Beside me, I saw Ari turn to the bookcase and reach up. But I was concentrating on my reading and didn't think anything of it.

Then, all at once, the class seemed to erupt. Kids squealed and burst out laughing. The sound was so loud and so sudden, I gasped in surprise. Kids roared with laughter.

And then I felt something tickle the back of my neck. And my cheeks suddenly felt prickly. My hair itched. I slapped at it—and pulled a spider off my head.

My mouth opened in a scream—but no sound came out.

I turned and saw Ari, grinning, holding the empty glass case in his hands.

And I knew . . . I knew he had poured the spiders over my head.

My skin itched all over. I felt the spider legs prickle my skin . . . my neck . . . my forehead . . . spiders scuttling through my hair . . . and now raining onto my shoulders.

I was covered in them!

"We only did it to help you!" Ari said. He had to shout over the laughter that rocked the classroom.

Help me?

"Noooooo!" I protested. Slapping at spiders, ripping them off my face, I ran through the laughter, out the classroom door, and down the hall.

He didn't do it to help me.

Of course, I knew that. It was late afternoon, and I was hunched in an armchair in my Me-Cave, thinking about what Ari and Lindy-Sue did to me. Picturing it again and again. Grumbling and mumbling and reliving it as it went on a loop through my mind.

My face still itched. And I could still feel the prickle of spider feet in my hair.

"They didn't do it to help me," I told myself. "They did it to embarrass me in front of everyone."

And everyone in the room thought it was a riot. Even Ms. Macy was laughing.

Well . . . I'm not the kind of guy who likes to get

revenge. I never think about paying people back or teaching them a lesson they'll never forget. Or anything like that.

I told you, I like peace and quiet, the quiet I have in my own private apartment.

But I'm afraid Ari and Lindy-Sue had gone too far this time. Putting a spider in my salad could be thought of as a joke. But dumping a case of twenty or thirty spiders on my head in front of my entire class isn't a joke. It's an act of war.

So what did I do?

I texted them both and invited them over for Saturday.

Lindy-Sue called me back right away. "I thought you were mad at us," she said.

"I was mad," I confessed. "But not anymore. How about a truce?"

She hesitated. "A truce?"

"Sure," I said. "Let's put an end to this spider thing once and for all."

A pause. Then she said, "You really mean it?"

"Tell you what," I said. "If you and Ari come to my house on Saturday, I'll show you something special. An awesome surprise."

"You'll show us your Me-Cave?"

"Maybe," I said. "Maybe I will."

And that's what I did.

I spent Saturday morning in my little apartment, working on my collection, getting everything ready for guests. And when Ari and Lindy-Sue showed up at my house, I didn't wait. I led them to the garage and unlocked the door.

"I can't believe we're finally getting to see your secret place," Ari said.

"This is way cool," Lindy-Sue said. "We won't tell anyone about it, Van. We'll keep your secret."

"Don't worry about it," I said.

I pulled open the door and pushed them inside. Then I slipped in behind them and slammed the door shut.

"Hey—it's totally dark," Lindy-Sue said. "Van, turn on a light."

I told you, there are no windows. And I made sure the ceiling light was off.

"We can't see anything!" Ari exclaimed. "It's pitch-black. What's the big idea—?"

There was silence for a long moment.

Then the two of them started to complain and their voices got all shaky and frightened.

"On my face . . ." Lindy-Sue said. "Something brushed my face."

"Hey—get off me!" Ari cried. "Something touched me. Whoa—something sticky . . . it . . . it's on me."

"I—I'm tangled in something," Lindy-Sue stammered. "Van—help us. What's happening? Turn on the light."

So I clicked on the ceiling light.

And they both screamed when they saw the spiderwebs. The long tentacles of web hanging down from the ceiling, webs as tight and thick as ropes.

"Ohhhh . . . get me out . . ." Lindy-Sue moaned as a long, thick strand wrapped around her waist. "It's sticky . . . Ohhh, it's sticky."

"Van, please—" A fat cobweb stretched around Ari, wrapping him up.

"How do you like my collection?" I said. "Here comes the best part."

I raised my eyes as the spiders came sliding down on their slender threads. Hundreds of them—my special collection—sliding down to greet the new arrivals. Spiders thick as rain.

"No, please! Please!"

"Let us go!"

They both struggled and squirmed. The webs wrapped around them. The spiders rained down.

As I watched, they both started to spin. They shot out their arms and spun harder, faster, like two tops.

They uttered cries as they broke free. They burst out of the garage and ran screaming down the driveway.

I watched them run down the street, screaming the whole way. I could still hear them two blocks away.

"Well, guys, now you know my secret," I said. "You know my thing about spiders? You had it all wrong. I'm not *scared* of spiders. I LIKE THEM TOO MUCH!"

THE GHOST IN
THE WALL

When I was a kid, I was always afraid.

Afraid of the dark. Afraid something evil was hiding in our basement. Afraid of getting lost. Afraid of the creaks and groans in our house late at night.

One thing I *wasn't* afraid of was finding a ghost behind my bedroom wall.

I guess I just never thought of it.

But I thought of it when I wrote this story. And I scared myself all over again!

"STOP TALKING ABOUT GHOSTS, JOE," MOM SAID. "WE'RE IN A brand-new house. A fresh start for all of us. Please try to stop worrying about ghosts."

I started to answer her. But the moving guys were rolling a couch into the room, and I had to dodge out of their way.

I backed into a large poster covered in brown paper that was leaning against the wall. Mom grabbed my hand to keep me from falling on it.

The new house was bright and sunny and much bigger than our old house. I was glad we were moving, but I still had a lot to worry about.

"Mom, you know ghosts don't have to stay in the same place. If a ghost is haunting you, it can follow you from house to house."

"Save that for your comic book," Mom said. She pulled

open a large moving carton. It was filled with cups and saucers.

I like to draw. I'm pretty good at it. I've been writing my own comic book. It's called *Stormy Wether, Ghost Chaser*. My character, Stormy Wether, is a superhero who can see ghosts.

Mom and Dad are always asking me to come up with another character. They say my comic book isn't helping me with my ghost problem.

"We've been over this a hundred times. You think our old house was haunted," Mom said, closing the moving carton. "It was old and run-down and creaky. But this house was just built. Some of the paint isn't even dry. We're the first ones to live in it. There can't be any ghosts here, Joe."

I sighed. "Mom, our house was *definitely* haunted. It wasn't just creaky. I told you, the ghost knew my name. Late at night, I heard it whispering: *"Joe . . . Joe . . . Joe . . ."*

"That was me," Dad said. He walked into the room carrying a tall table lamp. He set it down on the floor beside the couch. "I talk in my sleep."

I rolled my eyes. "Haha. Funny," I said. Dad thinks he's a comedian. I beg him to take me seriously about the ghost that haunted me, and he just makes jokes.

"Your room is almost finished," Mom said. "Why don't you go upstairs and move everything where you want it?

Your drawing table is there, too. You can start a new comic book."

"Okay," I said. I turned and started to the stairs.

"Don't touch the banister," Dad said. "The wood stain is still wet."

"And try to smile," Mom said. "This is an exciting day for us."

I raised my fingers to my forehead and gave her a salute. "Aye, aye, captain," I said. "Any other orders?"

They didn't answer. They were dragging cartons against the wall.

My new bedroom wasn't finished, but it was already awesome. It was big enough for a double bed. And my drawing table and a desk for my laptop fit perfectly under the two tall windows.

I checked out the closet. It was narrow and deep. I pulled the chain but the ceiling light didn't go on. Maybe it didn't have a bulb yet. I had to talk to Mom and Dad about that. *No way* I could have a dark closet in my room.

The walls were wood panels painted pale blue. Plenty of room to put up my superhero posters. The carpet was dark blue. My favorite color. I even had my own bathroom.

I found my drawing pad in one of the unopened moving cartons against the wall. I sat down and tried to sketch the beginning of a new Stormy Wether story.

But I guess I was more excited than I realized. I couldn't

concentrate. My brain was spinning with all kinds of thoughts. I put down my pen and went downstairs to see if I could help my parents unpack.

That night in my new bed, I couldn't get to sleep. My eyes were wide open, and I gazed at the shifting shadows on my bedroom ceiling.

And listened.

Listened for sounds of a ghost.

My old house was noisy at night. Creaks and cracks and groans. And whispers. Tonight, only silence. The new house was so quiet, I could hear the hum of the refrigerator in the kitchen downstairs.

Finally, my eyelids began to feel heavy. My eyes closed and I could feel myself falling . . . falling into a peaceful sleep.

"OHHHHHH!"

I uttered a frightened scream and jerked straight up when a deafening *craaaash* shook the house.

I leaped out of bed, tripping over the blanket. I staggered to the bedroom door and out onto the landing. "Mom? Dad?" My voice was hoarse from fright.

Their bedroom is downstairs. I could hear them in the living room. Lights flashed on. I straightened my pajamas and started down the stairs.

"Oh." I forgot about the banister. It was still sticky.

They both turned to me as I burst into the living room. "It's okay," Mom said. "No worries, Joe."

Dad had a large poster in his hands. "It fell off the wall," he said. "I guess I didn't hang it properly this afternoon."

I stared at the poster. The glass was cracked across the front.

A chill ran down my back, and I shivered.

"Did it fall? Or did a ghost pull it off the wall?" I said, my voice just above a whisper.

Mom raised a hand. "Joe. Stop!"

"That's just the kind of thing a ghost would do if he didn't want us in the house," I said.

Dad shook his head and frowned at me. "I knew I didn't use a big enough picture hanger when I put it up this afternoon. You've got to stop the ghost talk, Joe."

"Go back to sleep," Mom said, pointing to the stairs. "You're going to need your rest. Your cousin Mandy is coming to stay for a few days."

"Mandy? Oh noooo," I groaned.

They both squinted at me. "You have a problem with Mandy? You two have always been close."

I groaned again. "Close? She's horrible to me! She knows I'm afraid of ghosts. She does everything she can to scare me. She never quits."

"A little teasing never hurt anyone," Mom said.

"Maybe you can haunt each other!" Dad said.

Haha. He's a riot.

"Tell you what," Mom said. "I'll talk to Mandy. I'll tell her you're nervous being in a new house, and she should go easy on you."

"That won't help," I said. "She loves to torture me. It's her hobby."

Sure enough, when Mandy's dad dropped her off the next morning, she walked into the house. And what was the first thing she said to me? "Hey, Joe, is this house haunted, too?"

The kitchen wasn't unpacked yet. So we all went out to a pancake restaurant for breakfast. Mom asked Mandy what she was doing this summer.

"Going to sleepaway camp," she replied. "I'm totally psyched." Then she turned to me. "I can't wait to sit around a campfire at night and tell ghost stories."

"Joe is going to art camp for two weeks," Mom told her. "They give drawing lessons every day and also painting."

Mandy grinned at me. "Are you still drawing that funny ghost comic?"

I choked on a chunk of pancake. "It's not funny," I muttered. "It's serious."

Back home, Mandy unpacked her bag in the guest room across the hall from me. Then she demanded a tour of the new house.

"Okay," I said. "We can start in my room."

She glanced around. "Nice and sunny," she said. "Those big windows. And it's so much bigger than your old room."

"I'm going to put up my posters on this wall," I said. "And Mom and Dad are going to build me a bookshelf for the other wall."

She pulled open the closet door and peered inside. "Creepy," she said. "A ghost could hide in here."

"Please don't start," I said.

She pulled the chain. "Ooh, the light doesn't work. A creepy closet. It's so deep and dark. Dark as night. Joe, aren't you afraid?"

I didn't answer. I knew she was doing her usual thing. I started to the bedroom door. "Let me show you the rooms downstairs."

But she had turned to the wall. I watched as she ran her hand along the wood panels.

"Wow, look at this," she said. She tugged one of the panels to the side. "Joe, check it out. A loose wall panel. A ghost could slip in and out of here. Easy."

"Stop it!" I shouted, waving my fists. "Stop it! Please!"

A grin spread over her face. She was happy that she made me lose it. She slid the panel back into its place.

"Sorry," she said. "Don't be upset. I'm sure that ghost from your old house didn't follow you here. I mean, what are the chances?"

Mandy stopped at my drawing table and picked up the new comic book I had just started. "Stormy Wether?" she asked. "Who thought up *that* name?"

"I did," I said. "Put it down. I just started it."

She read the first two pages, shaking her head. "No wonder ghosts hate you, Joe. This guy goes around killing ghosts?"

"Stop talking about ghosts," I said. "Come on. I'll show you the rest of the house."

I led her down to the basement. "It isn't finished," I said. "It's just a basement. But Mom and Dad are going to build a game room down here. We're going to have Skee-Ball and air hockey."

"What about Foosball?" Mandy said. She ran a hand along the smooth concrete wall. "This is awesome, Joe. Your old house didn't even have a basement. Just that crawl space that was definitely haunted."

"Let's go back upstairs," I said. "Maybe we can find the carton with my posters in it and—"

I stopped because Mandy had bent down and was studying the floor in the corner. "Whoa," she murmured.

I stepped up behind her. "What is it?"

"Whoa," she repeated. "Check this out." She pointed.

"I don't see anything," I said. "Oh. Yeah. What is that?"

We were both staring at a puddle in the corner of the floor. Some kind of wet, green goo.

Mandy stuck a finger in it. "Thick," she murmured. "It's very thick. And look how shiny it is. I know what it is."

"Tell me," I said.

"Ectoplasm," she answered, staring hard at it. "Ghosts leave ectoplasm wherever they go."

"Mandy, please—" I started.

"You're the ghost expert," she said, standing up. "You have to know ectoplasm when you see it. There was a ghost here, Joe. Definitely."

I wanted to scream and punch the wall. But what good would that do? Would it make Mandy stop all the ghost talk?

"It's cleaning fluid," I said. "That's all. Just some spilled cleaning fluid. The builder cleaned every inch of this house before we moved in."

She shrugged. "Go ahead. Believe what you want, Joe. But don't believe your own eyes."

Back upstairs, we helped Mom and Dad unpack a few cartons. After lunch, Mom and Mandy went shopping for camp outfits. I went to my room to work on my Stormy Wether comic book.

Every few minutes, I looked up and gazed at the loose panel in the wall. Mandy had ruined my new room for me. I knew she was just trying to scare me. But I couldn't stop thinking about the loose panel and how a ghost could slip behind it easily.

After dinner, my parents drove us to a carnival that had set up in a park across town. Mandy and I went on some rides that were kind of babyish. But we didn't want to make my parents feel bad.

We had cones of pink and blue cotton candy, which left my face and hands sticky. And we played some dart and ring-toss games. Mandy won a little teddy bear. She gave it to a little girl who came walking by.

Then she grabbed my arm. "Check it out, Joe. A haunted house."

Eerie organ music blared out from the creepy-looking building covered in shadows at the back of the park. The windows were dark. The entrance was draped with thick spiderwebs. On a loudspeaker, a man's voice barked evil laughter, over and over.

"No way," I said. "Sorry. I'm not going in there."

"Too scary for you?" Mandy replied.

I nodded. "Yes. I'll have nightmares. I already have nightmares all the time."

She sighed. "Then how about the Hall of Mirrors?"

Two rows of tall mirrors were set up across from the haunted house. "Okay," I said. "I can handle funny mirrors."

I led the way. "Where is everyone?" I didn't see anyone going through the rows of mirrors.

"They're all on the rides," Mandy said.

The two rows of mirrors seemed to go on forever.

Mandy and I stepped in front of the first one and laughed. The mirror was curved so that we looked two feet tall. The next mirror stretched us so we appeared tall as giants.

We followed the row of mirrors as they curved in a circle. Each mirror was distorted in a different way. I stopped and stared into a mirror where my reflection was repeated over and over. There I was, getting smaller and smaller, stretching into infinity until I disappeared in the distance.

I turned to show this one to Mandy. "Hey—Mandy? Mandy?"

I didn't see her.

I squinted down the row of mirrors. I could see my reflection, big and little, stretched and squeezed. But no Mandy.

"Hey—Mandy!" I called. "Where did you go?"

No answer. All I could hear was the noise of the carnival in the distance.

I started to call her again—but stopped. Something caught my eye. I blinked. A face in the mirror.

Not my face. Not Mandy's face.

I moved to the next mirror. Yes. A slender, shadowy face. Peering out at me from the mirror.

I spun around. "Hey—!" No one behind me. No one else in the row.

But when I turned back to the mirror, the face was there. Gazing out at me. Not blinking. Not moving.

I moved to the next mirror. The shadowy face was still there. Right above my reflection.

I stepped to the next mirror. Then the next. The face—it was in each one!

With a cry, I spun away and started to run. There was no one else around. How could the face be watching me from every mirror?

"Mandy! Mandy!" I screamed her name as I ran. My shouts rang off the tall mirrors.

I nearly ran into her at the exit. "Hey! There you are!" she said. "I lost you. So I came out here to wait for you."

"S-someone," I stuttered. "Someone watching me."

She squinted at me. "Watching you? Where?"

"Inside the mirrors," I said, still breathing hard.

She laughed. "I get it, Joe. Now you're trying to scare *me*!"

"No! I'm serious," I said. "The face followed me. I—"

"Okay, okay," she said. "Take a breath. We can go back on the kiddie rides."

"I—I think I'm done with the carnival," I stammered.

Mom and Dad drove us home. It took a long while for my heart to stop pounding in my chest. I kept seeing the shadowy face staring at me from inside the glass.

Is there really a ghost following me?

Mandy said good night and went into her room across the hall from me. I stepped into my room, clicked on the ceiling light—and screamed.

My comic book. Pieces were spread all over the carpet. The comic had been ripped to shreds.

I grabbed some ripped pages and ran to tell Mom and Dad. They called Mandy into the den.

"Mandy, a joke is a joke," Mom said. "But this time you've gone too far."

Mandy stared at the torn pages in Mom's hand. "I . . . I don't know what you mean," she said. "Is that Joe's comic book?"

"You know it is," I said. "Totally ripped up."

Mandy shook her head. "I don't understand. You think I did it?"

"Yes. Who else?" I snapped.

"I didn't do it, Joe." She raised her right hand. "I swear. It wasn't me."

"Mandy, you need to tell the truth," Dad said.

"I . . . I was at the carnival with you. When would I do that? And why? I'd never do that. It's too mean."

Mom and Dad stared at her, studying her face. Mom turned to me. "I think she's telling the truth."

"But—but—" I sputtered.

Dad yawned. "Let's talk about it again in the morning," he said. "I'm sure we can figure it out."

Of course, I couldn't get to sleep that night. Every time I closed my eyes, I saw the ghostly face in the mirrors.

Yes. Ghostly.

And I couldn't stop thinking about my comic book. If Mandy didn't destroy it . . . who? There was no one else in the house besides Mom and Dad.

Or was there?

I kept gazing at the clock on the wall. It was nearly two in the morning. My eyes started to feel sleepy. I could feel myself falling asleep.

"*Joe . . . Joe . . . Joe . . .*"

The whispers forced me awake. I opened my eyes with a gasp.

"*Joe . . . Joe . . .*"

"Who's there?" I cried.

I heard soft laughter. So low I could barely hear it.

"Mandy? Is that you? Stop it!" I cried. "You're not funny!"

Silence.

Pale moonlight washed into my bedroom. I sat up straight and gazed around slowly. Shadows seemed to slide across the carpet as I watched. But there was no one there.

"*Joe . . . Joe . . . Joe . . .*"

The whispers seemed to be coming from the wall. I lowered my feet to the floor and crept across the room. My heart started to pound. My hands were suddenly ice-cold as I grabbed the loose wall panel.

I slid it away from the wall and peered behind it. No.

No one there. No ghost. Nothing. My hands trembled as I pushed the panel back into place.

I climbed back into bed, but I couldn't fall asleep. I lay there wide-eyed and alert, gazing at the ceiling, waiting for the whispers to return.

The next morning at breakfast, Mandy swore her door was closed the whole night. "I went right to sleep and didn't wake up until morning," she said.

She gazed at me across the table. "Sorry you had a bad night, Joe. Maybe you're just jittery being in a new house."

"I'm not jittery," I said. "Someone is trying to frighten me."

"Well, it isn't me," she insisted. "Dad is picking me up after breakfast. I'm going home early. Maybe it will stop after I leave. But it wasn't me."

I wasn't sure I believed her. I like Mandy, but I was glad to see her leave. Maybe the scares would leave with her.

A few hours after we said goodbye to her, a moving truck pulled into the driveway. Two movers in blue uniforms lowered our piano from the truck and rolled it into the living room.

Mom paced back and forth with her hand on her chin. "I'm not sure where to put it," she said. She pointed. "Maybe that corner? Or maybe . . ."

The movers were very nice. They rolled the piano all

around the room for her till she decided to put it next to the fireplace.

I went up to my room to start a new comic book. I sat down at my drawing table and took out my pens. I was thinking hard about how to start the new Stormy Wether story. But then something caught my eye.

The loose wall panel stood tilted at an angle. Did someone move it?

I crossed the room and slid it to the side. I peered into the space behind it. Nothing there.

I slid the panel back into its place and started to my drawing table. "Whoa." What did I hear? Was that water running?

I hurried out of my room. Yes. Water running in the bathroom at the end of the hall. I pulled open the bathroom door—and gasped.

Water gushed from the faucet. The tub was full and overflowing. Water poured over the side, puddled on the floor, and spread over the room.

I dove for the handle. Splashed through the puddle. Shut the water off.

"Mom! Dad! A problem!" I screamed.

Then I remembered. They both went shopping. No one else home.

The warm water soaked my socks. I splashed to the door and into the hall. I started to the linen closet across the hall. My plan was to pull out large bath towels to soak up the water on the floor.

I was halfway down the hall when the music started.

Piano music. Very loud. Some kind of classical tune.

But no one else is home!

The thought froze me. I stood there for a long moment in my soaked socks. Then I turned and raced downstairs, taking them two at a time.

The pounding music stopped as I burst into the living room.

"Huh?" No one there. No one at the piano. No one in the room.

"Mom? Dad?" I knew they weren't home, but I screamed for them anyway.

"What is going on?!" I cried out loud.

The water running in the tub . . . The loud piano music.

I gasped again as the ceiling lights started to flash. "Oh nooo!" A deafening shrill siren blast made me cover my ears. The security system!

Suddenly, I couldn't breathe. I couldn't think straight. Wave after wave of panic rolled down my body.

I stood there with the lights flashing and the siren blaring. And I stared in horror as the living room windows began to slide up and down.

Haunted. I was right. I knew it. The new house was haunted.

I had to get away from the noise and the flashing lights. I turned and ran up to my room. I slammed the door shut behind me. And stood there, hunched over, struggling to catch my breath.

My worst nightmare.

I raised my eyes to the wall. It was glowing! A shimmering green light. The ghost. The ghost was in there.

I couldn't hold myself back. I lost it. I stormed to the wall, raised both fists—and pounded as hard as I could on the glowing green light.

"What do you want?" I screamed. "I know you're in there. What do you *want?*" I pounded till my fists hurt. "Why are you haunting me?"

"I'll tell you why," a voice replied. A crackling, dry voice from inside the wall.

I started to choke. I stopped pounding and staggered back. "Wh-why are you haunting me?" I stammered.

"Because it's your turn," the ghost answered.

"Huh? What? My turn to do *what?*" I cried.

"Your turn behind the wall, Joe. I've haunted you for years. Now it's your turn."

"But—but—" I sputtered. "But I'm not a ghost!"

"Yes, you are," the crackling voice replied. "Your parents—they're afraid to tell you. But you *are* a ghost, Joe. And it's your turn."

"No! No!" I cried. "No! You're lying! You're—"

I felt an invisible hand grab my shoulder. It tightened . . . tightened till I screamed. The loose panel slid open. And I was pulled behind it. Pulled into the wall. The panel slid shut.

Now I'm the ghost in the wall!

"But . . . what do I do now?" I cried. "Who do I haunt?"

"Joe, calm down," the ghost whispered. "Just think of all the fun you'll have the next time Mandy comes to visit!"

THE THIEF

Several years ago, my wife and I were on vacation at a large beach hotel. We were having a terrific time relaxing on the beach and swimming in the warm ocean.

One night, we joined several people staying at the hotel and made our way to a special beach. Tucked in the tall grass, we saw hundreds of sea turtle eggs. It was the night when the turtles hatched and made their way to the water.

An amazing sight.

I remembered that night when I wrote this story. And I asked myself, "What would happen if someone stole a turtle egg and brought it home? Could something really scary happen?"

MOM WALKED INTO MY ROOM WITH A BIG SMILE ON HER FACE.
Her eyes flashed behind her red-framed eyeglasses. "Carlo, are you ready to see something amazing?"

Something amazing? I knew it had to do with science. That's because my mom is a science freak. Science is her hobby, and it's also her job. Her name is Dr. Fran Boyle, and she is the director of the Cape Cod Science Foundation.

So, even when we go to the beach to swim, she digs little creatures out of the sand and finds strange rock formations and shells to show me. How many twelve-year-olds like me know ten different kinds of mollusk? I do, because of my mom.

I climbed out of bed. I always do homework in bed. "What are you going to show me?" I asked.

"Sea turtles," she said. "I'm taking you to Nantucket Sound. To the sea turtle nesting grounds."

I squinted at her. "Turtles have nests?"

"They deposit their eggs high on the beach, back by the tall grass and reeds," she explained. "And tomorrow night the turtle eggs will begin to hatch."

"Baby turtles?"

She nodded. "Hundreds of them, Carlo. It's an awesome sight to see them crack out of their shells and scamper to the water."

"Wow," I said. "That sounds amazing." I raised the iPhone I'd been scrolling through. "When the turtles hatch, I'll make a video of it and share it in school."

Mom blinked. "Where did you get that phone?"

"I borrowed it from my friend Steven," I answered. "He said I could have it for a few days. I'm learning how to do movie trailers on this app called iMovie."

Mom gazed at the phone. "He loaned you his phone? Carlo, is that true? You didn't just take it, did you?"

"No way," I said. "I'm not doing that anymore. I swear."

She studied the phone in my hand for another long moment. Then she turned and started from the room.

"Mom, can I invite Kira to come watch the turtle hatching, too?" I asked.

Kira lives next door, and she's my best friend from

school. Our families spend a lot of time together. Kira and I are like twins, except we're not.

"Of course," Mom answered from the hallway. "Kira always enjoys our science trips."

The next night after dinner, Kira was in my room. We were waiting for Mom to finish a business call so she could drive us to Nantucket Sound.

Kira picked up the iPhone from my dresser. "Did you get a phone? You didn't tell me."

"No. I borrowed it," I replied. "I'm practicing iMovie so we can start that movie we want to make."

Kira and I are both into sci-fi monster movies, and we want to make one of our own. I told you, we're like twins.

Kira sighed. "My dad says maybe I can have a phone for my birthday," she said. "But that isn't for three months."

I could hear Mom still talking on the phone downstairs. "I'm going to make a video when the turtles start cracking out of their shells," I told Kira. "It's kinda like science fiction, right?"

She didn't answer. She picked up a book from my bedside table. "Hey," she said, turning to me. "I've been looking everywhere for this book. Is it mine?"

"Oh. Sorry," I replied. "I thought you were done with it."

She pressed her hands against her waist and frowned at me. "You just took my book and didn't ask me?"

"Guess I forgot," I said.

Mom stepped into the room. "Ready to go? It's a full moon tonight. That will make it easy to see the eggs as they hatch."

It was a warm summer night. No clouds above. Tiny twinkling stars and a full orange moon still floating above the trees.

The beach is a short drive from our house. Mom took her favorite route through Mashpee National Wildlife Refuge. Believe me, she and I spend a lot of time there exploring and studying birds and other animals. I could be a tour guide.

A line of cars was parked on the road behind the water. Mom pulled our SUV in at the end. "Word gets around when the turtles are about to hatch," she said. "It has become a very popular event. It gets more crowded every year."

We climbed out of the car and began to walk to the tall grass at the shore. People were talking softly as they walked.

"Think the turtles like such a big audience?" Kira said.

Mom put a finger to her lips. "No. We have to be very careful not to disturb them." She pointed to the phone in my hand. "No flash, Carlo. Turtles are very sensitive to light. No noise and no lights."

We joined the crowd of people huddled in the tall grass. Several people had brought folding beach chairs. Others were on their knees, peering onto the beach.

Mom pointed. "See how the eggs are all nestled at the edge of the sand? The mother turtles aren't moving. It's as if they are guarding their eggs."

There were hundreds of eggs. They all glowed like Christmas tree lights under the bright moonlight. The big turtles kept moving their heads from side to side, as if they were on guard.

"This is way cool," I whispered.

Kira slid the phone from my hand. "Hey, Carlo, tell me again. Where did you get this phone?"

"I told you. I borrowed it. From Steven. He loaned it to me for a few days."

She narrowed her eyes at me. "He did? Really? I saw him looking for it in school. He was really upset."

"Uh . . . maybe he forgot he loaned it to me."

Mom put a finger to her lips again. "Shhhhh. Check it out. Those eggs over there. They are cracking."

A hush fell over the crowd. No one moved or whispered. A lot of people had their phones raised, ready to take photos or videos.

I heard soft cracking sounds. Very soft, then getting

louder. Several eggs shook as they split open. Tiny legs pushed out from the breaking shells.

"Awesome," I whispered to Kira. I took the phone back from her and started to crawl forward.

"Where are you going?" Kira whispered.

"I want to get closer for my video," I whispered back.

I slid between two people at the edge of the grass and raised the phone. Tiny turtles were bursting from their eggs. They didn't hesitate. They scrambled on wobbly legs, slipping and stumbling, making their way to the water.

I held the phone higher to try to capture the whole scene on the video. There were so many of the tiny creatures, it looked like an ocean wave rolling to the sea.

I moved closer, close enough to touch some of the mother turtles. Eggs cracked all around them. They followed after the newborn turtles, making sure they reached the water.

"Awesome," I heard Kira tell my mom. "An amazing sight. Thank you for bringing me."

"I knew it was something you would never forget," Mom told her.

I stopped recording and slid the phone into my pocket. Then I turned and walked back to Mom and Kira. "Totally great, Mom," I said. "It was just like being in a nature documentary."

We talked about it all the way home. When we returned

to the kitchen, Mom said she'd make some popcorn. "We can have some snacks and watch Carlo's video," she said.

Kira followed me up to my room. I clicked on the light and closed the door behind me.

"Why are you still wearing your jacket?" Kira asked. "Did you forget we're indoors now?"

I raised a finger to my lips. "Shhh. Don't say a word."

I reached into a jacket pocket and pulled out an egg. "Look what fell into my pocket," I whispered.

Kira gasped. Her mouth dropped open. "Oh no. Carlo, you didn't. You stole a turtle egg?"

"It's not stealing," I said. "No one owns them." I cradled the egg between my hands.

"But—but—" Kira sputtered.

"I took the biggest egg I could see," I said.

"But why?" she demanded. "You promised you would stop taking things, Carlo. You promised—"

"I'm going to make a video when it hatches. You know. For extra credit."

Kira shook her head. "But if your mother finds out . . ."

"She won't," I said. "I'm going to hatch the egg in the bathtub. In the guest bathroom at the end of the hall. No one ever goes in there."

I rubbed the smooth shell. It was heavy, heavier than a normal egg. And it felt warm. I shook it. I could hear something bouncing inside.

"Stop that!" Kira cried. "What are you trying to do?"

"Just testing," I said.

"The baby turtles need water," Kira said. "They need to be outdoors. With their mother turtles. You can't—"

I waved for her to follow me. Holding the egg carefully in one hand, I led the way to the guest bathroom at the end of the hall. I clicked on the light and handed the egg to Kira. Then I leaned over the tub and started the hot water running.

I waited till about an inch of warm water covered the bottom of the bathtub. Then I turned off the faucet and held my hand out for the egg.

Kira dropped the egg into my hand. "This isn't right, Carlo. How do you know—?"

"It's a science experiment," I said. "Just like my mom does." I lowered the egg into the water. Then I stood up and dried my hand off on a towel.

"What if the turtle hatches during the night, and you miss it?" Kira asked. "Are you going to stay up all night to watch it?"

I shook my head. "I'll leave the bathroom door open. I'm a very light sleeper. I'll hear the egg cracking if it hatches."

Kira opened her mouth to speak. But Mom's shout from downstairs interrupted her. "Come on down, you two. Popcorn is ready."

We turned and started down the stairs. "What were you two doing up there?" Mom asked.

"Science," I said. "The turtle hatching was so exciting, I wanted to do more science experiments."

That night, I dreamed about turtles. There were a hundred little turtles in the dream. For some reason, they were in my bed. I tried to pull up my blankets, but the turtles covered them, climbing over me, over my chest and onto my face.

When the turtles totally covered me, I woke up. I shook the dream away and listened hard. Was that a cracking sound coming from the bathroom down the hall?

No. I recognized the sound of tree branches creaking in the wind outside my window.

I woke up early the next morning and leaped out of bed. I raced down the hall to the bathroom to see if anything had happened during the night.

No. The egg rested right where I had left it, at the end of the tub in an inch of water. "Why are you such a slowpoke?" I asked it. Most of the other turtles had hatched at the same time last night.

It was Saturday morning. Kira appeared at the kitchen

door while I was having my breakfast cereal. Mom opened the door. "You're up bright and early," she told Kira.

"I want to help Carlo with his science experiment," she said. She kept her eyes on me.

"Nothing happening yet," I said.

"Are you going to share your experiment with me?" Mom asked, filling her coffee mug.

"It's top secret," I said. "We'll tell you all about it when we know it's a success."

She took a sip of coffee and smiled. "I'm so happy you were inspired by last night."

Kira rolled her eyes, but Mom didn't see it.

When we went up to the bathroom, something was definitely happening in the bathtub. The egg had rolled to the center of the tub. And I heard *scratch scratch scratch* from inside the shell.

I was down on my knees at the side of tub. Kira leaned over me. "It's ready to hatch. Are you excited?" I asked her.

"Not as excited as you," she replied. "You're so excited you forgot the phone. I thought you wanted to make a video."

I slapped my forehead. "Thanks for reminding me. I climbed to my feet and darted to my bedroom. I grabbed the phone and raced back to the bathroom.

Craaaack craaaack.

Jagged cracks appeared in the shell. Kira was on her

knees now, leaning over the tub. I could see the egg shaking and rolling from side to side in the shallow water.

"Oh, wow!" I cried as a leg poked out.

Is it a leg?

I raised the phone to my face, set it to video, and pressed the start button.

Craaaack.

Another leg appeared. The two legs wiggled in the air. Kira and I squinted hard at them. They didn't look like baby turtle legs. They looked like smooth pink sausages.

"This is awesome!" Kira cried. She leaned farther into the tub.

Another long *craaaack.*

The egg rocked hard. It bounced in the water. And the whole shell fell away.

Kira and I both screamed. A small creature splashed up and down. It had six pale, pink sausage legs. A round body like an octopus. Three black dots for eyes. Two slender antennae on top of its bulb of a head.

"Oh nooooo!" Kira wailed, her eyes bulging. "Carlo— *it's NOT a turtle!*"

She jumped to her feet. We both stumbled back from the bathtub.

The phone fell from my hand and clattered over the tile floor.

The three dot eyes on the creature's head kept blinking. The two antennae waved rapidly from side to side.

It had a tiny slit of a mouth, and the mouth kept opening and closing, making wet, slurping sounds.

The six legs splashed water against the side of the tub. They stretched from the octopus-shaped body, which pulsed in and out.

"I don't believe it . . . I don't believe it . . ." Kira had her hands pressed against her cheeks. She kept repeating that over and over, her eyes bulging from her head.

"Believe it," I said. I leaned closer to the tub. "What's all over its body?" I squinted hard. "I—I think they're suction cups," I stammered. "That's what they look like. Little suction cups all over it."

The creature made a groaning sound as it stretched its body and legs across the water.

How did it fit in that little egg?

Or is it growing before our eyes?

It was already bigger than a hamster or chipmunk. Maybe the size of a seagull.

Kira and I both gasped as it kicked hard at the sides of the tub, sending water splashing over the edge. "Is it . . . trying to get out?" I cried.

The creature bounced against the tub, and the suction cups made popping sounds. The slit of a mouth made spitting noises.

"What is it? What *is* it?" Kira cried.

"I've never seen anything like it," I replied.

"It—it's like out of a movie or something," she stammered. "Why did you do it, Carlo? Why did you steal the egg?"

I shook my head. "I—I don't know!" I stammered. "Just for fun. I picked this egg because it was a little bigger than the others."

With a hard splash, it pressed its body against the side of the tub. The suction cups made popping sounds as they stuck to the porcelain. The six legs pushed the body higher.

"It's going to get out," Kira said. She gave me a push. "Get your mom—quick!"

"But—but—" I hesitated.

She shoved me again. "We need her, Carlo. Hurry. Get your mom!"

I ran down the hall and took the steps two at a time. "Mom! Hey, Mom!" I shouted for her as I burst breathlessly into the kitchen.

"Mom?"

Not there.

I turned to leave when I saw a handwritten note on the kitchen table. I grabbed it in a trembling hand and read it quickly.

EMERGENCY at the lab, Carlo.

Had to run out. Sorry. No time to tell you.

I'll be home as soon as I can.

I stared at the note. "Mom, we really need you," I muttered.

I can text her, I decided.

My heart pounding, I rocketed back up the stairs.

"Carlo—hurry! Please!" Kira's shout rang down the hall.

I dove into the bathroom. "Oh nooo!" A cry escaped my throat.

The creature had grown. It was the size of a large cat!

The legs were reaching over the side of the tub. The terrifying *pop pop pop* of the suction cups made me cover my ears.

"Wh-where's your mom?" Kira stuttered.

"Not here," I said. I reached for the phone on the floor and raised it to my face. The screen had shattered. Jagged cracks all over it. A chunk of glass had fallen out.

Would it still work?

I pressed the *on* button. The screen remained blank. I pressed again. Nothing. I jabbed my finger all over the screen. Solid black.

"Not working," I said. "It's broken. Maybe we should—"

I didn't finish my sentence because the creature hoisted itself over the side of the tub and hit the floor with a heavy *thud*.

The body plopped wetly on the tiles, then bounced back up on four of its legs. The three eyes gazed up at me.

"Let's get out of here!" Kira cried, tugging my arm. "We can lock it in the bathroom till your mom gets home."

Breathing hard, I stared down at it. What could it be? What kind of animal that looks like that hatches from an egg?

I shouldn't have wasted time asking those questions. I should have run, as Kira said.

Too late. The creature bounced up on two legs. It bumped into me, knocking me backward. It wrapped four legs around my thigh and pressed its suction cups into my jeans.

"Nooo! Heeelp!" I screamed and tried to pull it off. But the creature had a hard grip, squeezing my leg and climbing higher.

I tried to kick it away. But it didn't budge. I kicked and squirmed and tried to slam it against the wall.

"Get it off me!" I shrieked. "Get it *off*!"

Kira backed out of the bathroom. "No way! I'm not touching it!"

"But it's squeezing my leg!" I wailed. Hopping on one leg, I tried to kick it back into the bathtub. But the creature held on tight, clinging to my leg.

"Can you walk?" Kira demanded. "Can you drag it outside?"

"Huh? Outside?"

She nodded. "If we can get it to the pond at the back of your yard, maybe it will swim away or something."

"But—but—" I sputtered. "We can't just let it loose. If other people find it—"

"Let's worry about that later," she said. "Do you really want it to squeeze your leg off?"

The suction cups made *popping* sounds as the creature inched up toward my waist.

"Okay, okay," I said. "I'll try to walk. But it's heavy. It already weighs a ton. OUCH!! It *bit* me!"

I took a step forward, dragging the leg with the creature attached to it. Kira took my hand and helped pull me into the hall.

Four of its legs were wrapped around my thigh. The two front legs waved up at me. Was it trying to tell me something?

I dragged my leg to the stairway. I gripped the banister to keep from falling over and slowly carried the creature down the stairs. Kira helped pull me into the kitchen. Mom still wasn't home.

We made it out the back door, and I started over the grass, dragging the heavy beast. We had tall seagrass and shrubs at the back of our yard. Beyond that, a small, oval-shaped freshwater pond.

"Owww." My leg ached up and down. The creature's four legs tightened as if it were clinging on for dear life.

"What if it doesn't like to swim?" I said. "What if it isn't a water creature?"

Kira started to answer. But she stopped and uttered a cry as a shadow fell over us.

A tree! A tree stepped into our path!

We both stopped. I stared at the wide, dark trunk. Then I raised my eyes way up to the top of it.

"Oh no," I moaned. It wasn't a tree.

It was another six-legged monster. At least twelve feet high. Its six legs as wide as tree branches. Three shiny black eyes as big as soccer balls. Staring down at Kira and me.

Before I could move, the giant beast took a thundering step forward. The creature bent low. Two arms shot out and ripped the little creature from my leg.

The giant lifted the little monster in the air. Its wide mouth made sucking sounds as the giant creature held the little one up to its face. Then it tucked the little one into a pouch on its middle—like a kangaroo mother.

A shadow fell over Kira and me again as the tall monster leaned over us.

"P-please—!" I stuttered. "Please don't hurt us!"

I wanted to run, but my legs wouldn't move. Kira grabbed my shoulder and gazed open-mouthed at the enormous monster.

We both uttered a cry as its top legs snapped forward. I made a choking sound as it forced something into my mouth. Some kind of pill? It tasted sour as it slid down my tongue.

Kira gagged as a pill went down her throat.

"Those are language pills," the big creature said. "They translate from my language to yours."

Kira and I exchanged glances. The creature made harsh sounds like a dog growling. *But I could understand every word it was saying.*

"Please—" I started again.

"You shouldn't have stolen my baby," the monster said.

"We didn't know," Kira replied. "We thought it was a turtle egg."

The creature growled. "After I came to Earth," it said, "I hid my baby's egg in the safest place I could find. I hid it with all those other eggs so no one would discover it."

"You—you're from another planet?" I stammered.

The monster's growl shook the trees. "Do I look like I'm from Cincinnati?"

It made a joke.

"We didn't know," Kira said. "When Carlo stole your egg, he thought it was a turtle. Please accept our apology."

"Are you . . . going to let us go?" I asked.

The monster made a rumbling sound. "Let you go? I can't."

"Wh-what do you *mean*?" I shrieked.

Two arms stretched toward us and wrapped around Kira and me. The arms pulled us to the creature's sides.

Its heavy footsteps flattened the grass as it began to walk, carrying us with it. "You must come with me now."

At the far side of the pond, I saw a tall metal structure. It looked like a twenty-foot-tall trash can. A door slid open on the front.

"It . . . it's a spacecraft," Kira muttered.

"No! You can't take us!" I cried. "You can't!" I tried to squirm free. But the creature's grip was too tight.

"Please don't! Please don't!" Kira and I both screamed.

But the big creature shoved us both through the open door of the spacecraft. Then it moved quickly to block our way out.

"Nothing personal," it said.

"Huh?" I cried. "Nothing personal? What does that mean? Why are you taking us? Why?"

"Just doing my job," it answered.

"Your job?" I said. "What is your job?"

"I'm a thief."

A BAD BIRTHDAY PARTY

When I turned ten, I had a very bad birthday party.

My mom burned the cake, so we had to have cup-cakes from the supermarket. Two boys from my class got into a fight, and they both ended up with bloody noses. Three of my friends said they were sick and couldn't come.

And then my cousin Stanley thought it would be funny to give everyone a scare. He pulled a black wool ski mask over his face and climbed into the house through the front window.

Everyone thought he was a robber. Terrified kids went screaming out of my house.

That was a bad party.

I remembered it when I wrote this story about an EVEN BADDER party!

AT THREE O'CLOCK, THE BELL FINALLY RANG. I'D BEEN WATCHING the wall clock over Mr. Trevor's head for over an hour. *Tick . . . tick . . . tick . . .* Why does the clock move so much slower on Friday?

I jammed my books into my bag, jumped up from my desk, and followed the stampede to the classroom door. "See you all Monday," Mr. Trevor called. I don't think anyone answered.

"Hey, LeShaun, wait up!" I called. LeShaun sits in front of me. We're not really friends, but we try to make each other laugh when the class gets boring. Like every day. I'd like him to be my friend for real.

He turned and lowered the phone he had to his ear. "Jimmy, what's up?"

I had to shout over the voices and laughter and slamming lockers up and down the hall. "Want to come over and hang out? I have the new updated version of *Morbid Fantasies* on Xbox."

He shook his head. "Sorry. Not today. I . . . uh . . . have a thing."

A thing?

I tried not to look disappointed. "Oh. Okay. Catch you Monday," I said.

He raised the phone to his ear. As I walked away, I'm pretty sure I heard him say into it, "No, I'm not doing anything. Want to hang out?"

I stepped out of the school and made my way past the teachers' parking lot. The afternoon sun was a big red-yellow ball low in the sky. Blinking, I pulled my sunglasses down. My eyes are very sensitive. I'm a lot more comfortable in the dark.

I'm kind of lucky. My dad owns the Drexel, the only movie theater in town. It's the darkest place you can find. And, of course, I get in free whenever I want.

I saw Maria Handy walking across the grass. She was struggling with two bulging brown paper bags, one in each arm. Maria is the equipment manager for the cheerleaders. I always see her carrying big packages to practice after school.

I thought maybe I could help her. Truth is, I have had a major crush on Maria since fourth grade.

I trotted up beside her. "Here. Let me take one for you," I said. I reached out both hands to grab a bag.

Maria jumped to the side. The bags nearly slid from her arms. "No. That's okay," she said. "I'm okay, Jimmy. Someone is picking me up."

Someone?

"No. Really—" I said. I made another grab for a bag.

She spun away. "No problem. I've got this," she said. "But . . . thanks anyway." She hurried away, fumbling the bags as she walked.

Typical. Totally typical.

I'm Jimmy Lupo, and I may be the loneliest kid in Greever Falls. I'm not sure. But I definitely know I'm lonely.

And I know why.

I'm not going to talk about it. It's *hard* to talk about it. But I know why I'm lonely. I know why I spend so much time in my room, playing *Morbid Fantasies* on the Xbox by myself.

I was a block from home, thinking about LeShaun and Maria, when I heard running footsteps behind me on the sidewalk. "Hey, Jimmy—wait," a voice called.

I turned to see Lucy Wolfe waving as she ran after me. I stopped and waved back at her. A smile crossed my face. I was instantly cheered up.

Lucy is maybe my only friend. That's because she's my cousin. And our families are really close. And Lucy and I grew up together since we were tiny babies.

She stopped and tossed back her long black hair and

wiped sweat off her forehead with the back of one hand. "Didn't you hear me calling to you?"

I shook my head. "Sorry. I was thinking about . . . things," I replied.

"How many times have I told you not to think? It will only get you in trouble."

I rolled my eyes. "Haha. You're so funny. What's that you're chewing?" I pointed.

"It's a beef stick." She chewed off a chunk. "Want one?"

"For sure," I said.

She reached into her fanny pack, pulled out a stick, and handed it to me. We both chewed as we walked to my house.

No one home. Mom and Dad never get back till after six.

"Do you want to watch me play *Morbid Fantasies*?" I asked when we were in my room.

"I'd rather shave my eyeballs," Lucy said.

She makes me laugh. I never can tell if she's serious or not.

I sat down on the edge of my bed and picked up the game controller. Lucy sat cross-legged on the floor and chewed her beef stick.

"Hey." She bumped my leg. "I didn't see you at Courtney Varner's birthday party Saturday. Where were you?"

I sighed. "Courtney had a birthday party? I didn't know. I wasn't invited."

She lowered her eyes. "Oh. Sorry. I thought she invited the whole class."

I stared at the blank screen. I suddenly had a heavy feeling in the pit of my stomach. "She invited everyone but *me*?" I murmured.

"It was a bad birthday party," Lucy said. "The pizza was ice-cold. And Will Munroe got sick and threw up on the presents."

I slammed my fists on the bedspread. "I don't care if it was a bad party. I'm so totally bummed. No one invites me to a birthday party. Ever."

I jumped to my feet. "I'm so sick of it, Lucy. I'd like to have some friends—you know?"

She motioned for me to sit down. "I know how you feel, Jimmy. But we both know what the problem is. What can you do about it?"

"Nothing," I muttered.

"I'm your friend," she said.

"That doesn't count. You're family," I said. "Do you have another beef stick?"

She searched her bag. "No. No more. Come on. You don't want to spoil your appetite before dinner."

I rolled my eyes again. "Thanks, Mom. You know I can never spoil my appetite no matter how hard I try."

She laughed. "True."

"What are you doing this weekend?" I asked her.

"I'm going to the car show at the convention center with Amy Stone and her brother."

"Can I come, too?" I asked.

Lucy stared at me for a long time without answering.

"Oh, I get it," I said. "Forget I asked. That's okay, Lucy. I know why you don't want me. It's Amy and her brother, right? They wouldn't want me there."

She stared at me a while longer. "Maybe you and I could go on Sunday," she said finally. "I don't mind going a second time."

"That's okay. Forget it," I said. "I'm not into cars anyway. And I'm on a really hard level of *Morbid Fantasies*. It's going to keep me busy all weekend."

Lucy climbed to her feet and started to the door. "I've got to get home," she said. "Listen, don't get down on yourself, Jimmy."

I snorted. "What does *that* mean?"

At dinner, Mom had a surprise for me.

She passed the platter of lamb chops to me. I had already eaten two, but I still felt hungry. I took two more chops and passed the platter to Dad.

"Jimmy, you're not doing anything this weekend, right?" Mom said. She knew the answer. She didn't wait for me to reply. "Well, I made a plan for you."

I set down my fork and knife. "A plan?"

"Well, I ran into Lucas Franklyn's mother at the gym. She said Lucas didn't have any plans, either. So I made a date for you to go over to Lucas's house Saturday afternoon. You know. Just to hang out with him."

My mouth dropped open. My breath caught in my throat. "You did *what*? You made a *playdate* for me?"

Mom wiped her mouth with her napkin. "You don't have to call it that, Jimmy."

"A playdate? Like I'm in kindergarten?" I screamed.

"Don't shout at your mother," Dad said. "We both want to help you."

"*Help* me? Help me?" My voice came out high and shrill.

"We know you want to make friends," Mom said. "There's no harm in me giving you a little head start. I know Lucas is in your class and—"

"How embarrassing is this?" I said. "My mommy is going to take me to a playdate. Will there be cookies and milk? Will Lucas and I play *Chutes and Ladders*? Will there be *Play-Doh*?"

"Jimmy, please," Dad said. "Indoor voice. Okay?"

"Mom, how could you—"

"I'll just drop you off," she said. "I'll stay a block away. I won't even come near the house. You'll be happy. Who knows? Maybe you'll make a new friend."

I took a deep breath. I was ready to shout some more.

But then I had a new thought. Maybe this wasn't such a bad idea.

I knew Mom was just trying to be helpful. She knew how unhappy I've been. And she was trying to do something about it.

I took another deep breath. "Okay," I said. "Let's give it a try. Thanks, Mom."

Dad grinned. He had lamb chop juice all over his chin. He likes it when I'm polite to Mom.

In school, I went up to Lucas at a table in the lunchroom. The chair across from him was empty. "Is this seat taken?" I asked. I started to lower my lunch tray to the table.

"Yeah. Someone is sitting there," he said.

I glanced around the crowded room. I didn't see anyone heading to the table. But I raised my tray and started to walk away. "See you Saturday," I said.

Lucas squinted at me. "Saturday?"

Maybe his mom hasn't told him I'm coming over, I thought.

I found an empty table in a corner of the room and sat down to have my lunch.

Saturday afternoon, Mom drove me across town to Lucas's house. He lives on the North Side of Greever Falls, where all the fancy houses are.

"What did you bring?" Mom asked, glancing at the stack of books in my lap.

"It's my Morbid Fantasies graphic novels," I answered. "I thought maybe Lucas would like to look at them with me."

"Terrific idea," Mom said. "I'm glad you're getting behind this plan."

"Well . . . maybe I can get him into the game, too," I said, "and he and I can play it together online."

Mom pulled the car to the curb and pointed out the windshield. "That's the Franklyn house over there."

The big stone house stood at the top of a wide, sloping lawn. I saw a row of tall windows all around, black shutters, and several chimneys. Two blue SUVs were parked in the long, curving driveway.

I opened the car door and started to climb out. "Have fun, Jimmy," Mom said. "Call me when you're ready to be picked up."

I could feel my heart start to flutter in my chest as I made my way up the cobblestone walk to the front door. I'd known Lucas a long time from school. But I had never been to his house and I never hung out with him.

I stepped onto the front stoop and raised my finger to press the brass doorbell. But the door swung open before I could push it.

"Hello. Are you Jimmy?"

Lucas's mom stared out at me through the screen door.

I nodded. "Yes. Is Lucas—?"

"Didn't you get my message?" she said. "Lucas is sick. He can't have any visitors today."

I made a gulping sound. "Sick? Really?" I tried to hide my disappointment.

"Very sorry," she said through the screen door. "Sorry you didn't get the message. Another Saturday, maybe?"

"Yeah. Okay." I backed off the stoop. "Uh . . . tell Lucas I hope he feels better."

"I will," she replied, and the door closed with a loud *thud*.

I turned and started to walk back down the cobblestone path. Something in the front window caught my eye. I squinted against the sunlight and saw Lucas and two other kids from school. They were pressed against the window, watching me walk away.

"Jimmy, you can't get revenge on every kid in school," Lucy said. "Besides, people don't get revenge. That's only in movies and on TV shows."

"I don't want revenge," I said. "I want to teach everyone a lesson."

We were in my backyard, sitting in the shade of a wide, old oak tree. Lucy had brought beef sticks. But I was too stressed and excited to chew one.

"You want to teach *everyone* a lesson?" she said. "Everyone?"

"Just those kids who are mean to me," I said. "The kids who won't be my friend."

"That's just about everyone!" Lucy said. She laughed, but I didn't think it was funny.

I grabbed a beef stick from her bag and bit off the end. "Lucas was the last straw," I said, scowling at the ground. "When I saw him in class yesterday, he pretended to cough. So I would believe he was really sick last Saturday."

"What a creep," Lucy murmured. "So, what are you thinking, Jimmy? I know you. I know you already have a plan."

I chewed for a while. "For sure I do. I'm going to have a bad birthday party."

Lucy's mouth dropped open. "Excuse me? What is a bad birthday party?"

"You'll see," I said.

She bumped my arm. "No. Really. What are you thinking?"

I nodded. "It's my thirteenth birthday in two weeks. I'm going to have a big party and invite everyone in class."

Lucy choked on her beef stick. I waited for her to stop coughing. "That idea is no good," she said. "Know why? You can invite everyone in class, but no one will come."

"I thought of that," I said.

She stared at me, waiting for me to explain.

"Dad says I can have the party at his movie theater. We can have the whole theater all to ourselves."

"That's cool," Lucy said. "But I still don't understand—"

"We're going to show the *Morbid Fantasies* movie," I told her. "Dad got an early copy. No one anywhere has seen it. It will be special for my birthday party. And everyone will want to see it."

Lucy thought about it. "Maybe . . ." she said finally.

I could feel myself getting pumped just describing my plan. "The kids will all come to see the movie," I said. "They can sit in the dark and they won't have to talk to me or be friendly or anything. And then . . ."

"Then what?" she asked.

"A big surprise," I said. "I'll promise a big surprise for everyone at the party."

"Hmmmm." I could see Lucy was thinking hard. "It's a bad idea," she said. "It won't work. No one will come."

I jumped to my feet. "They'll come," I said. "I know they will. They'll come for a free movie no one in the world has seen. And because it will be dark, and they won't have to talk to me. You'll see!"

Lucy sighed. "Guess it's worth a try. Don't worry, Jimmy. I'll be there in case no one else comes."

Lucy was wrong. Everyone came. My whole class.

Kids had been waiting months for the *Morbid Fantasies* movie. They *had* to see it, to be the first ones ever to see it.

And I knew they were all curious about the big surprise I promised in the invitations. Some of them probably thought some stars from the movie would appear.

But, of course, that wasn't the surprise.

I watched them all make their way down the aisle of the totally dark theater. Groups of friends sat together. They filled the front rows, talking and laughing, holding their big bags of popcorn and chewing on long candy bars.

I knew what a lot of them planned. They planned to watch the movie, then hurry out of the theater before there was birthday cake or presents or anything. They planned to leave before they had to talk to me.

But I had a surprise for them.

Kids cheered when the movie came on. The screen was suddenly so bright, glaring against the deep darkness of the theater. I had my dark glasses on. But the glow from the screen still hurt my eyes.

I watched the movie from the back row of the theater.

I had waited a long time to see it. But I couldn't concentrate. I kept thinking about my big surprise for everyone.

I tried. I tried to be friends with you all, I told myself. *You can't blame me. You can't blame me for my big surprise.*

The movie seemed to take hours and hours. Kids clapped and cheered. They were loving it.

I paced back and forth along the back wall, trying to keep calm, trying to force my drumming heartbeats to slow down.

Finally, the movie ended. The closing credits came on. Kids cheered and clapped. A few of them started to stand up.

Lucy appeared at my side. "Jimmy, what are you going to do now?" she asked.

"My big surprise," I said.

She tugged at my sleeve. "What is it? Tell me."

"I'm going to turn all the lights on," I replied.

"No!" she cried. "No—Jimmy—don't!"

Too late.

I was standing in front of the switch on the wall. I shoved it up with one hand, and all the ceiling lights flashed on. Kids shielded their eyes. The theater was bathed in light—brighter than day.

Lucy followed me to the front. Kids were blinking and rubbing their eyes.

"Surprise, everyone!" I shouted.

I pulled off my sunglasses and tossed them away. I could feel the fur growing on my face. Feel the thick, bristly fur roll over my arms, sprout over my hands.

My fangs poked over my lips and drool ran down my chin.

And once again, my belly rumbled and growled. I felt the hunger. The incredible, sharp, painful hunger.

You see, I knew what my problem was in school. I knew why kids didn't like me, why they didn't want to be my friend.

I knew they didn't like me because I'M A WEREWOLF!

But even a werewolf needs friends.

Kids were screaming, racing up the aisle, struggling to open the theater doors.

I raised both fur-covered arms and howled at the ceiling. Just to let them all know that I was coming.

"Hungry . . . So hunnnngry . . ."

Drool pouring over my fangs, I turned to Lucy. "Better hide your eyes," I growled. "This is about to become a bad birthday party, a *very* bad birthday party."

WHAT'S IN THE CLAW MACHINE?

When my son Matt was a little guy, we used to take him to local carnivals that popped up. At one of the carnivals, he discovered a claw machine.

You've probably seen one. A glass case filled with prizes. You have to move a long metal claw, pick up the prize you want, and drop it down a chute to collect it.

Matt had his eye on a small rubber football. He was determined to grab it. Each try cost twenty-five cents.

He moved the claw over the football and lifted it up. But each time he tried to carry it to the chute, the football dropped out and fell back to the bottom of the case.

He tried again and again. It was becoming a very expensive football!

Finally, we realized the claw was broken. Matt could never win his prize.

When I started this story about a claw machine, I thought: What if the machine wasn't just broken? What if it was *evil*?

THERE ARE ONLY TWO KIDS WHO TRAVEL WITH THE PACKER Brothers Circus, and I'm one of them. I'm Mary-June Rice, but everyone calls me MJ. I'm twelve, and I've been a circus kid my whole life.

That means living in a trailer, traveling year-round from city to city. Before she married Dad, my mom was a teacher. So, she home-schools Teddy Packer and me in our trailer.

Teddy is the other circus kid. He's my age and, yes, he's a Packer. His family owns the circus, and his dad, Renaldo Packer, is the ringmaster.

Mr. Packer has a booming voice and struts around in his red-and-gold costume with his tall ringmaster hat, and everyone treats him like a king. Which he is. He's king of the circus.

Sometimes his son Teddy tries to act like a prince. But

I do my best to keep Teddy from getting too obnoxious. Which is a tough job.

Teddy likes to get on my nerves by hopping up and down and scratching his belly and going, "Ooh ooh ooh," like a chimpanzee. He thinks that's a riot because of my family's circus act.

Rices' Famous Chimps.

My grandfather started the act many years ago and Dad keeps it going. We have six funny, lovable chimps, and Dad has trained them to do a terrific trick.

What's the trick? He trained them *not* to obey his commands.

When the act is in the ring, Dad will shout to them, "Run through this hoop!" And the chimps sit on their stools and don't move. And then Dad yells, "Jump up and down and then do a cartwheel." And the chimps just sit there looking at one another. They don't move.

"Everyone climb the ladder!" Dad orders. And the chimps don't move.

It doesn't take the audience long to figure out what's going on here. And they begin to laugh harder and harder at each trick the chimps don't do.

Rices' Famous Chimps really is a famous act, especially among circus people and people who like to go to the circus.

We take great care of the chimps. We treat them like family.

I spend hours with them. I like helping out with them because I know someday the act will be mine.

They are all gentle and sweet and playful. But Ozzie is my favorite.

Ozzie loves when I give him neck and shoulder massages. He closes his eyes and coos like a bird. He loves the attention.

Ozzie is a banana freak. Every time I give him a banana, he goes wild. He tosses his head back and howls and does a triple cartwheel.

The other five chimps are awesome, too. But Ozzie is special.

The chimps all make lip-smacking, good-night-kiss sounds when I tuck them in for the night. It's so funny.

One night, Teddy appeared when I was tucking them into their trailer. "MJ, you're done with work, right? Let's go to the carnival."

The carnival has ring-toss games and dart games and shooting games. Also a few rides and a sideshow. It travels with the circus.

"I'm not in the mood," I said. "I don't want to win another goldfish. I don't know where to put them."

"Since when do you win anything?" he said. "I win all the prizes. When it comes to the games, you lack only one thing."

"What's that?" I asked.

"Skill." He laughed.

He's always telling me what I lack.

Outside the trailer, I heard music and applause from the show tent. The performance was still on. But people jammed the carnival aisles, too.

"Okay, I challenge you to the balloon dart-throwing game," I said.

He shook his head. "No way! Last time you almost took that guy's eye out. Remember?"

"You pushed my arm, Teddy."

"I did not!" he cried. "The guy had to duck. He thought you were aiming the dart at him. He begged you to go play some other game."

Teddy pulled my arm. "You have to come. Dad says something new came in for the arcade. And he wants us to check it out to see if it's ready for the public."

I thought about it for a moment. "Okay," I said, "if I can bring Ozzie."

Ozzie perked his head up when he heard his name.

Teddy frowned at me. "You know your dad doesn't like it when you take the chimps out."

"But Ozzie has been bored and restless," I replied. "He needs a night out."

Teddy hesitated. "Well . . ."

"He's a good boy," I said. "He won't get in any trouble."

Teddy shrugged. "Okay. Let's go."

Ozzie practically leaped into my arms.

We stepped down from the chimp trailer. I held Ozzie's hand as the three of us walked away from the show tent.

Lights from the Ferris wheel washed over the carnival aisle. A little girl dropped her cotton candy cone on the pavement. I scooped it up for her before she had a chance to cry.

"Follow me. The new arcade attraction is over here," Teddy said.

Rifles popped in the duck target-shooting game.

"A new game?" I asked.

He shook his head. "Not a game." He pointed to the arcade hall. "Over here."

Holding on to Ozzie's hand, I followed Teddy past a row of pinball machines. He led me to a tall glass machine in the corner. Swirling white light flashed all around it.

"A claw machine," Teddy said. "Awesome!"

I stared into the wide glass case. The bottom was filled with dozens of large clear plastic eggs. There was a different prize in each egg. I saw balls and yo-yos and rubber lizards and big dice and Rubik's Cube games and flashlights and magic tricks and miniature fruit and little stuffed animals.

Ozzie pressed his face against the side and gazed in, too. I think he had his eye on an egg with a plastic banana inside.

I told you, he's a banana freak.

A claw—like the claw at the end of a steam shovel—stood at the top of the case. It was raised on a long metal arm.

Teddy grabbed the two silver controls at the front of the case. "You turn these wheels and try to get the claw to pick up a prize," he said. "Then you drop the prize down this chute."

I gave him a shove. "I wasn't born on Mars, you know? I've seen these things."

He laughed. "I don't know what you've seen, MJ. You're like me. You've been in the circus your whole life. You spend all your time with chimpanzees . . ."

"Chimpanzees and you!" I said. I bumped him out of the way and grabbed the two control wheels. Ozzie stood close beside me, gazing into the case.

"Okay, Teddy. Let's give this a try. How much money do you have to put in?"

He grinned. "We can do it for free." He pulled a key from his jeans pocket. "My dad gave me this key. I turn it on the side of the machine, and we get free play."

"Awesome," I said. I pointed to a plastic egg. "See that little mermaid doll with the flashing eyes? That's what I'm going to grab."

"Good luck," Teddy said. "I don't think it's so easy." He took his key and slid it into a slot on the side of the case and turned it.

The machine hummed to life. The sound made Ozzie hop up and down excitedly.

I spun the controls and the claw moved in a circle at the top of the case. It took me a little while to figure out which wheel made it go up and down and which wheel made it move from side to side.

I kept my eye on the egg with the little mermaid doll.

Two little kids came rushing over, trailed by their parents. They wanted to pet Ozzie.

I shooed them away. "Not now," I said. "This is intense. I'm trying to grab a prize."

The parents didn't look too happy. But they herded the kids away.

I lowered the claw over the eggs . . . slowly . . . slowly . . . Swung it over the mermaid doll egg. Dipped it.

And missed.

"It's not as easy as it looks," Teddy said, laughing.

Ozzie made a grumbling sound. I think he could tell I was getting tense.

I swung the claw to the left, then started to lower it slowly. "Yes!" I cried when I made the claw wrap around a plastic egg.

I gripped both wheels tightly. "I've got one, Teddy," I said.

"Carry it to the chute on the side," he said.

Slowly, I swung the claw to the right side of the case.

Carefully, I lowered it over the opening. Carefully . . . Carefully . . .

"Oh no!"

The plastic egg slipped out of the claw and dropped back onto the other eggs. They made a rattling sound as the egg settled to the bottom.

Teddy laughed again. "Close one, MJ."

I turned to him angrily. "You think you could do better?" I snapped.

"Of course," he replied. He stepped around Ozzie, bumped me out of the way, and took the control wheels.

He lowered his face to the glass. "See that red squirt gun in the middle? Next to the little banana? It's already mine!"

He spun one wheel, and the claw swung from one side of the case to the other. Then he slowly moved the claw over the egg with the little squirt gun inside.

"Watch how a pro does it," he said.

He turned the wheel, and the claw started down. He moved the claw slowly, and we watched it inch lower. Then it stopped moving about three inches from the plastic egg.

"Hey—!" Teddy sputtered. He slowly turned the wheel. But the claw didn't move.

He spun the wheel the other way. The claw didn't budge.

"It's frozen," he muttered. "The claw is stuck."

"Keep trying," I said.

"I *am*. It's jammed. It isn't moving." He shook his head. "That's why Dad wanted us to check this out. These new machines never work right."

Ozzie made a *hoo hoo hoo* sound. He could tell something was wrong.

Teddy let go of the control wheels and pulled the key from his jeans pocket. He moved to the back of the machine.

"What are you going to do?" I asked.

"This key my dad gave me opens up the back," he replied. "I'm going to open it up and reach in and try to get the claw moving again."

"Don't take any eggs," I said. "That would be cheating."

He turned the key and opened the door at the back of the machine. "I'm not going to take anything. I'm just going to fix the claw."

I stared into the glass. I could see Teddy at the back of the case. I watched his hand reach into the machine. He wrapped his fingers around the long metal arm that held the claw. He moved it carefully up and down.

ZZZZZZZZ.

A loud, crackling buzz made me gasp.

A shock of electric current?

Teddy's arm and hand disappeared!

I blinked a few times, gazing into the glass. "Hey—where did you go?" I asked.

No reply.

"Teddy?" I called. "What happened? Did you get a shock? Why did you stop?"

No answer.

I started to the back of the machine. But something caught my eye. One of the eggs on the bottom of the case appeared to be bouncing up and down.

The eggs rattled and shook. And one egg bounced on top of them.

I bent down and squinted into the glass.

Then I let out a scream that echoed off the arcade walls.

"Teddy! Noooo! Teddy!"

I rubbed my eyes. I had to be imagining this. *No way. No way!*

Was I seeing things?

No!

Teddy . . . a *two-inch-tall* Teddy was on his knees inside the plastic egg. He was waving both arms at me. I couldn't hear him. But I could see he was red-faced and shouting.

"Teddy!" I screamed. "I see you! I see you! How—how did this happen?"

He shouted something and beat both fists against the side of the plastic egg.

"No! No!" I glanced around. The arcade was empty. No one around to help me.

I rubbed my eyes again. I kept thinking I was imagining this.

Teddy pounded his tiny fists against the inside of the egg. I could read his lips. He was shouting for help.

"I—I'm coming!" I said. "I'll pull you out."

I raised Ozzie's hands to the top of the case. "Stay there. Don't move," I told him.

Then I dove to the back of the machine. I leaned close and peered through the open door. I could see Teddy in his egg. He was beating his fists against the plastic, and the egg was rocking back and forth over the other eggs.

I started to reach into the machine, then jerked my hand back.

"Careful, MJ," I said out loud. "Don't touch the claw arm. You'll get a shock."

I knew I had to be careful. If I touched the wrong thing . . . could I end up like Teddy?

I'll just grab Teddy's egg, I told myself. *I won't touch anything else.*

Moving slowly, I slid my hand back into the machine.

Maybe . . . just maybe, he'd return to his normal size if I carried him back outside.

I moved my hand over the plastic eggs an inch at a time. Slowly . . . slowly.

My whole arm started to tremble. I realized I was holding my breath.

I spread my fingers and began to lower them over Teddy's egg. Slowly . . . Carefully . . .

My hand touched the plastic. My fingers curled around the egg, and—

ZZZZZZZZZZZ.

A bright white light pulsed in front of me, blinding me. I tried to pull my hand away. It wouldn't budge. I couldn't see it. I couldn't see anything.

My whole body crackled and buzzed as if an electrical current was holding me, swallowing me.

Gasping, I struggled to breathe.

Finally, the light faded. The buzzing sound came to a stop. I took breath after breath, blinking fast, trying to blink the shock away.

And when I could see clearly, I screamed. "TEDDY!"

"No. Oh no!" He pressed his hands against his face. "No. No way. MJ, you—you're in the egg with me."

I let out a cry. Was it *true*?

I beat both hands against the plastic. I gazed out at the other eggs all around us. I could see the red squirt gun and a tiny banana and a pair of pink dice.

Yes. It was true. Teddy and I—we were trapped in the same egg.

Teddy shut his eyes. His whole body shuddered. "We'll never get out of here," he whispered. "Never."

I tried to think of something to say. But I was too shocked and frightened to make a sound.

A grinding noise made me gasp. Something moved above us. I raised my eyes to the top of the egg—and saw the claw arm slide across the ceiling of the case.

"The claw is moving again!" I cried.

Teddy's mouth dropped open as we watched it swing from side to side. "What is making it move?" he asked.

I turned to the front of the case and saw the answer to his question.

Ozzie!

Ozzie had his hands on the control wheels. He gazed through the glass and spun the wheels.

"It's Ozzie!" I cried. "Ozzie is moving the claw!"

We stared out at the chimp. He seemed to be studying the eggs, peering in without blinking.

"He can save us," I told Teddy. "Ozzie can lift us out."

Teddy squinted out at Ozzie. "Do you think—?"

My heart pounding, I began to wave both arms at the chimp. I knew he couldn't hear us. But he could see us. And he could pick up our egg in the claw.

I knew he could.

Teddy began waving, too. We were both waving wildly.

We jumped up and down and made the egg bounce and roll.

"He sees us!" I cried. "I know he does. Look—he's gazing at us and moving the controls."

"Come on, Ozzie!" Teddy cheered. "Come on. Pick us up. You can do it!"

Above us, the claw arm swung rapidly to the left. Then it slowed down as it moved the metal claw right above us.

"He's doing it!" I shouted. "Look—he's doing it! He's going to pull us out!"

"Thank you, Ozzie!" Teddy screamed. "Thank you! You are saving us!"

We both stopped waving as the claw began to lower. I held my breath and watched it slide down. I didn't move. I didn't blink.

The claw dipped to the eggs. I saw it open, then close around an egg.

"Noooo!" I screamed. "Ozzie—that's the wrong egg!"

"No! No! Nooooo!"

Teddy and I both moaned in horror as the claw moved past our egg and lifted the egg beside us. The claw swung the egg to the open chute. Then dropped it down the chute.

The plastic egg came sliding into Ozzie's hands. He raised it to his face.

He held it in one hand and pulled it open with his other hand.

Then he tugged his prize from the open egg.

It was a banana. A small yellow banana.

Of course.

What else? Ozzie wanted the banana.

The chimp grinned at his prize. Then he tossed his head back and howled and did a triple cartwheel.